A Pattern of Murder

(A Spicetown Spin-Off)

A Carom Seed Cozy

Sheri Richey

For further information, contact the publisher: Cagelink

ISBN: 978-1-63752-149-6

Front Cover art by Mariah Sinclair

Carom Seed Cozy Mysteries

(A Spicetown Spin-off)

Murder All Sewn Up

Tailor Made Terror

A Fitting End

A Pattern of Murder

Romance by Sheri Richey:

The Eden Hall Series:
Finding Eden
Saving Eden
Healing Eden
Protecting Eden
Completing Eden
∞
Willow Wood
Knight Events

Chapter 1

Peggy's feet slapped the hot pavement of Paprika Parkway as Sully pulled her along by the leash. She had taken him out early for a morning walk today, hoping to beat the heat, but when she had to change her usual walking route, it put her in the direct sun.

Approaching Fennel Street, she saw Mayor Bingham sitting on one of the new iron benches outside Chervil Drugs, swinging her feet forward and back as she glanced over her shoulder.

"Good morning! Are you testing out the new bench?"

Startled, Cora Mae swiveled around in her seat and smiled. "Hi, Peggy! Yes, and this one is a little high for me." Cora's feet did not touch the ground. "I'm waiting for Ted to refill a prescription for me." Cora patted the seat next to her. "Give it a try!"

Sully greeted Cora Mae, and then Peggy sat down

beside her. "I would be in the air conditioning, if I could. It's already too warm for us." Sully's tongue hung out of the right side of his mouth, dripping saliva on the sidewalk as he panted. "We usually walk down Fennel Street because it's shaded, but we can't get by right now. If they don't clean this mess up by tomorrow, Sully and I are going to skip the walk altogether."

"I know. It's gone on too long. The Chief said he would check on things, but having a semi-trailer truck parked on Fennel Street for two days has not just been a headache, but I'm sure it's hurting everyone's business. Saucy told me he couldn't even walk by there to get to the bakery yesterday." Harvey "Saucy" Salzman liked his morning social at the Fennel Street Bakery every so often. He didn't go daily, but when the weather was nice, he liked to stop in for the camaraderie.

"I think everyone's business has been hurt. No one has anywhere to park. They drive down just to see what's going on, but when they can't park, they move on. I can't even see the bakery and I'm right across the street from it!"

"I'm surprised there hasn't been an accident. It's blocking the entire lane and you can't see around it." Cora Mae waved when she saw Chief Harris walking down the opposite side of the street with his dog, Briscoe, leading the way toward the new business. "There goes the Chief. Maybe he'll hurry them along."

Regina Adkins was opening a new dress shop in the storefront next to the Fennel Street Bakery called Sassafras. The semi-trailer truck had arrived yesterday to unload her merchandise and equipment. The sidewalk was littered with boxes and handcarts while several people walked in and out of the new store.

"Have you met the owner, Regina?" Peggy scratched the top of Sully's head. His breathing had slowed, but he needed water.

"I haven't, but it seems everyone else has. She's been in City Hall, but I must have been out at the time. I was planning to stop in and introduce myself, but I didn't want to bother anyone while they were moving. Dorothy said she's been in the Caraway Cafe almost daily, but I always miss her. Is she nice?"

Peggy's forehead creased as she searched for the proper word to describe a slightly pretentious middle-aged city person having a mid-life crisis. "She's different."

Cora raised one eyebrow and smiled. "I understand she's brought a group of employees with her. I guess she doesn't plan to hire local people."

"My understanding is that this group travels with her to set things up. Sometimes she leaves one behind to manage the place and the group moves on with her. This time she said she plans to stay and give small town life a try, so I assume she'll hire local people once they open."

"Interesting business plan." Cora Mae smirked. "Dorothy tells me the team she brought is mostly young people. I think they've come in the cafe. I wonder where they're staying."

"Oh, Clyde's got them scattered all over town." Peggy chuckled. Clyde Newman worked for Red Pepper Realty and had rented the storefront to Regina. He had also been helping her look for a permanent home, but in the meantime, he found temporary rental accommodations for the girls. "Regina is in the Nutmeg Inn, but the others are in rentals around town."

"Well, I'm sure I'll eventually run into them all."

"We need to be getting back to the store. Arlene will be missing us, and I think Sully needs to cool down." Sully got to his feet when Peggy stood.

"Okay, I'll check on Ted's progress. See you later."

Regina Adkins rushed down the sidewalk toward Conrad Harris as he approached. He saw Briscoe's tail and ears quiver with tension. "Whoa!" Conrad held his hand out to stop Regina and pulled Briscoe back to stand at his side. "You don't want to rush up on a police dog like that."

"Oh, sorry, Chief. I'll be careful." Regina calmed her voice and stayed several feet away.

"How's it going with this?" Conrad waved his hand

at the 18-wheeler blocking all access to the downtown community and the major east-west road through town.

"I know what you're going to say, Chief."

"You do?" Conrad's eyebrows rose and he tilted his head. "What am I going to say?"

Regina hesitated a moment. "You want to know when it's going to move."

"I know when it's going to move. You told me yesterday that it would be gone by noon today. Do you also know what I'm thinking? Or what I plan to do if it is still here at 12:01?"

"I know, Chief. It's taking longer than I thought. I haven't found a place to live yet, so I had them bring my stuff today so I can move it upstairs. I don't know if I'll like it up there or not, but it will be a place of my own for now."

"As long as the truck is gone by noon."

"But, Chief, I don't know if that's possible now. I hadn't planned to move my stuff in when we talked yesterday."

"I see two guys going in and coming out. Where are all the extra people you have working here? Why aren't they helping?"

"The girls are upstairs cleaning the living area for me. I don't think anyone's lived up there in ages and I can't unpack until it's cleaned."

Conrad huffed. "You can all clean house when the

rig is gone. Right now, you need everybody you have out here in this street moving these boxes inside because at 12:01 today I will ticket and tow this truck off Fennel Street. Do you understand me?"

"But you can't do that!" Regina advanced again and raised her voice.

Conrad pulled Briscoe close to lean him against his leg. "I can and I will."

Regina stepped back and huffed. "So much for the congenial small-town welcome."

"You had that welcome yesterday despite the fact that you systematically shutdown all of these people's livelihood without a single consideration for them at all. None of these storefronts can get any business because you are blocking the street and all the parking."

Regina looked down the street, avoiding Conrad's gaze. "I'm sorry."

"Don't tell me. Tell them. You owe them all an apology, and if you aren't going to be considerate enough to move that rig to the community center parking lot and carry your stuff down the sidewalk to your store, I will see that it gets moved myself."

"I'll take care of it, Chief."

Conrad nodded and turned Briscoe around to walk back to the station. They couldn't get down the sidewalk anyway and he had to start working on a plan to move an 18-wheeler. That situation didn't come up often in a small town and it might take at least a phone call or two.

Chapter 2

Peggy opened the door for Sully and glanced around the craft shop. Seeing no customers, she unhooked his leash and let him waddle back to the storeroom for a drink of water. "What did I miss?"

Arlene chuckled and nodded her head toward the street. "The little blond girl from across the street came over here wanting to borrow tape. I told her she needed to go down to the drugstore for that. She tried to argue with me that because we were a shipping store, we should have tape..." Arlene shook her head.

"Why in the world do they need tape? Everything is already taped up in boxes. If anybody has packing tape, it's probably the guys driving the moving van."

"Well, ten minutes later, the tall girl with dark hair came in wanting scissors. I showed her what we have, but our scissors are not for ripping into boxes. After she realized I wasn't loaning her a pair, she went down to Chervil Drugs, too."

Peggy laughed. "I hope they didn't run into each other down there. From what Regina said, those two don't get along well with each other."

"I didn't know that."

"Yes, she said when Clyde was trying to find them a place to stay, he suggested they share a vacant house that was for sale, and Regina said she put a stop to that idea. She was afraid they'd kill each other if they were left alone together."

"My goodness! I can't imagine working all day with someone you hated."

Peggy nodded. "Apparently, the little blond girl is difficult to get along with. I think her name is Eden."

"She looks really sweet, but I don't think she's too bright." Arlene winced at the harsh statement, but there was no kinder way to describe it.

"I ran into Cora Mae down at Chervil's. She said she was refilling a prescription, but I think she was spying on the Sassafras disaster. The Chief was headed over there to tell them to move that truck."

"It was there all day yesterday, how much more time does it take to empty? I didn't expect it to still be here today."

"Me either! I'm sure he'll take care of it." Peggy opened Sully's crate and he snuggled down in his blanket for a nap. "I had to walk down Paprika Parkway instead of Fennel Street when we were out on our walk, but when I walked by the Ole Thyme Italian, I saw JoAnne had a sign out front saying Stromboli is on special today. Now I can't get it out of my head."

"You should get some on your way home tonight!"

"I think I'm going to, but I'll have to run Sully home first to come back and pick it up. I can't leave him in the truck. I've been thinking about him lately and I think he needs to start staying at home during the day. I may have made a mistake bringing him with me every day."

"He's no trouble when he's here." Arlene glanced over and pointed. "He's already sound asleep.

"I know, but he's difficult to get in my truck now that he's so big. He sleeps half the day away and he could just as easily do that at home. I may talk to my neighbor, Daniel, and see if he'll check on him for me one day. I'd like to give it a trial run before school starts back for him."

Peggy jumped when the bells on the door jingled and Karen Goldman walked in with her head still turned to the street. "Good morning!"

"Hi, Karen." Arlene leaned on the checkout counter. "Are you off today?" Karen ran the Sweet & Sour Spice Shop on Ginger Street, just down the street from the Nutmeg Inn.

"No, but Donna's opening for me. I just dropped in

to get some floss. I was going to stop on my way to work, but I couldn't park anywhere. I just went to the store and walked over here. What's going on out there?" Karen hooked her thumb over her shoulder.

Peggy rolled her eyes. "Sassafras is moving in."

"At a snail's pace," Arlene added. "That truck was there all day yesterday, too."

"I admit, I don't have a lot of experience moving, but surely it can't take this long to unload!"

Peggy shrugged. "We can't see a thing over there, so I don't really know what they're doing. I think it left last night and came back today, but I don't know how much longer this is going to continue."

"So, what do you know about this Sassafras place?" Karen said in a hushed tone, although no one else was in the store. "Have you met them?"

"Yeah, they've all been over here at one time or another. The owner, Regina, says she is going to stay around, but the other people are just here to help her set up." Peggy pointed out the front window. "There's Regina. She's the one walking around the back of the truck."

"I'm still trying to learn all their names." Arlene touched her fingertips to her temple. "I can't keep them straight. Kim is older, so I remember her, but the other girls look like they are in their early twenties."

"Gretchen told me the other day that the young girls

were driving her crazy. The boss is staying at the Nutmeg Inn and the girls are in and out all the time to see her. I think they all get in the lobby together sometimes and they make too much noise." Karen glanced out the front window. "Growing pains, I guess. We want new businesses and progress, but it's difficult dealing with those unknown personalities sometimes."

Arlene pointed out the window. "There goes Regina. It looks like she's headed for the Caraway Cafe."

"A little early, isn't it?" Peggy looked at the clock on the wall. "Dorothy might be in there, but they aren't open yet."

"Regina will probably just bang on the door." Arlene grinned. "She's pretty bold."

"City folks." Karen sighed. "Well, I didn't come to gossip. Really, I didn't. I do need some floss. The color is number 420."

"What are you working on?" Arlene propped her elbow on the cash wrap and put her chin in her palm. "Is it a kit or an original creation?"

"It's very original and I'm really excited about it. I found this website where you could convert a photo into a cross-stitch pattern and I'm stitching a picture of the store! I plan to frame it and hang it up in the shop when it's done."

Peggy handed the floss to Arlene to ring up the sale. "I have some software that does that. I haven't used it in years, though. I should probably let people know that I can convert their pictures if they want a personalized pattern. I hadn't even given that a thought."

Arlene's eyes widened. "I can put that in our newsletter!"

Peggy chuckled as she pointed at Arlene. "Yes, you should do that."

Arlene had revived the sale email list and started creating a regular newsletter to send to Peggy's customers. Initially, it had been to share news of The Salty Shipper opening for business, but Arlene seemed to find an unlimited number of other things to share. She was now including free patterns, seasonal decorating ideas, and crafting tips in each edition.

"We'd love to see it when you're done!" Arlene handed Karen her bag.

Karen pulled the door open and looked over her shoulder. "I'll text you a picture, so you can't see all of my mistakes!"

Peggy laughed and waved as Karen pulled the door shut, but she could see a faraway look in Arlene's eyes. When she stared off into space with an unfocused look, it usually meant something had flipped her creative imagination. "What? What are you thinking?"

Arlene inhaled deeply and her thoughts poured out. "You know those paintings that Sonjay Wilson does of the streets of Spicetown? He has almost every storefront in town shown in one painting or another, and photographs of those paintings are online. I saw them after he sent several of them to town for that showing at the community center."

Peggy nodded. "They were very expensive!"

"Yes, but everyone loved them, even people who had never been to Spicetown." Arlene grabbed her mobile phone and her finger flipped through her saved photos. "We could print those pictures and you could convert them to cross-stitch. We could make a demo of each one and decorate the walls in The Salty Shipper with them and sell the patterns. We could even sell the display because your shipping customers aren't all going to be crafty, and then we would just make another!"

Peggy frowned in thought. "I was thinking about taking a picture of Sully and then making a pattern from it. That way, we could show the photo and the cross-stitch side by side, so patrons would know how it works. I think a lot of people might like a picture of their pet or their family."

"Another brilliant idea!" Arlene pointed a finger at Peggy and beamed. "You work on Sully, and I'll see what I can do with Fennel Street. These would make great gift ideas, too. I wish we'd thought of this earlier in the summer!"

The movement on the sidewalk caught Peggy's attention, and she saw Regina was headed their way. She glanced over at Arlene to see if she had noticed, and saw Arlene's stoic resolve set in. The workers at Sassafras had developed a pattern of asking for handouts up and down the street from all the merchants. Arlene had already had to rebuke two workers from Sassafras today. "Here comes strike three."

Chapter 3

"Good morning, girls!" Regina's cheesy smile was especially wide today. "How is everyone?"

Arlene busied herself behind the cash register without making eye contact because it was Peggy's turn to respond to Regina's demands.

"Good," Peggy said. "Are you about moved in now?"

Regina glanced over her shoulder and through the front window as if checking the view. "We are close to emptying the truck. The chief told us to have it gone by noon, and we are doing everything we can to make that happen."

"That's good to hear." Peggy nodded. "We'd sure like our parking back."

"Oh, I understand. The chief told me that this was a huge inconvenience for everyone and I promise you I never meant for that to happen. I'm so sorry it's taken so long."

Arlene looked at Peggy. "Maybe we'll have some customers this afternoon, then."

"Well, we appreciate the update." Peggy had learned the hard way never to ask Regina what she could do for her today, as she might a typical customer. Regina seemed to meet every question with a request for a favor.

"Oh, you're welcome! The reason I stopped by was to see if you gals have a refrigerator here. We're planning a little potluck celebration tomorrow for lunch and I don't have a refrigerator yet. We're just putting together a few snacks so we can work right through lunch and nibble as we go."

Peggy frowned. "Well, we have a small one, but it's full of stuff. How much room do you need?"

"Oh, just a corner or two. I thought I'd buy a lunch meat tray from the grocery store and maybe a cheese cake or some dessert. The rest would just be chips and bread that don't need to be kept cool."

"If the dessert can stack on the meat tray, we can probably fit it in." Peggy didn't see a way out.

"I told the girls they could bring something if they wanted. A couple of them do like to cook, but I don't think the housing they have right now provides any cookware. It's hard to live out of a suitcase for too long. I think we've eaten at all the restaurants Spicetown offers and we've run out of ideas."

"Paxton is nice," Arlene said, raising her head to participate. Regina had previously shared dismal reviews of her meals in Spicetown so far, and Arlene wasn't interested in hearing her friends being denigrated further. She could support sending the Sassafras team to another town. "It's not that far, and they have a wide variety of restaurants and lodging options."

Regina smiled. "We've talked about taking a trip over there this weekend, maybe Sunday. We don't all fit in one car, though!"

Peggy nodded, finding no way to end the conversation.

"Thank you both. I really appreciate the help. Vicki and Dorothy couldn't help because of the codes or something." Regina waved her hands in confusion. "Restaurants have to follow food handling codes. I don't know the details, but I'm planning to order us a couple of refrigerators once we get a little more settled. I'm hoping to move to the second-floor next week. Does anyone else on Fennel Street live above their store?"

"I don't think so." Peggy wasn't sure where Abby lived, but there were living quarters above the Spicetown Blooms & Gifts store. "There used to be a couple, but none that I know about now."

"Hmm, it may get scary down here at night then." Regina chuckled nervously.

"Nah, we don't have scary stuff too much around here. It will probably be quiet and peaceful because you won't have noisy neighbors." Arlene walked around the checkout counter and walked toward the doorway that connected the craft store to the shipping store. Looking busy hadn't made an impact, so Arlene was planning to just walk away from this conversation.

"I hope so! Oh, one more thing. I need some silk purple flowers. Is that something you can order easily or do I need to try Paxton?"

"We can get those. What kind of flower and how many?" Peggy reached for an order pad as Regina pulled a piece of paper from her back pocket.

"It's all here. You can keep this." Regina handed her the paper. "That's just a copy of an old order I did for another store. See you tomorrow."

Arlene turned in the doorway and listened for the bell on the door. "Is she gone?"

Peggy smiled. "Yes, she's gone. I guess I need to take some drinks out of the fridge and move things around a little. You know she's going to show up tomorrow with a full week's worth of groceries, don't you?"

Arlene shook her head. "It's always something with her. I've lost my patience with it." This had been going on now since Regina arrived and it had finally worn Arlene down. "What's the flower order look like? I can look at the online catalog for them."

Peggy handed Arlene the paper. "She's only got an hour left to move that truck. I'm anxious to see what the chief is going to do when she begs him for more time. She doesn't seem to think any rules apply to her, and that's going to rub Chief Harris the wrong way."

Cora Mae hung up her phone and saw her assistant, Amanda Stotlar, appear in her doorway.

"A call came in while you were on the phone and I took a message." Amanda handed a slip of paper to Cora. "It's the man from the railroad exhibit again, and he has questions about insurance bonds and security that I couldn't answer."

"Ugh," Cora scowled. "Mr. Abbott is being quite the pill. He's making me sorry I booked this display."

Amanda smiled. "He is a little curt on the phone."

"He's not any sweeter in person."

"We haven't advertised the event yet. You could cancel it." Amanda's eyebrows rose in encouragement. She hadn't worked on the tickets or promotion yet, and wouldn't mind marking those things off of her to-do list.

"That may end up happening because I can't seem to make him happy. I agreed to rearrange the stage because he didn't like the floor plan we have. Then, I agreed to hang the plastic shields and put up stanchions like we did when we had the paintings displayed. Now he wants guards posted." Cora threw her hands in the air. "I'm beginning to think he doesn't want to bring his display to Spicetown at all."

"Mr. Salzman would be disappointed if it didn't happen. He knows about it and he's excited."

Cora Mae sighed. She saw the twinkle in Saucy's eye when she had shared her plans to schedule the exhibit, and she hated to disappoint him. "I'm sure Saucy has told several people about it by now."

"Mavis is interested in seeing the display, too. She said she had some trains in her attic that she pulls out at Christmas. Her first husband was a collector and she keeps them so they can be passed down in the family."

"I haven't seen much of Mavis lately. Is she still working at the nursery for Bryan part-time?" Amanda's husband, Bryan, owned the Stotlar Plant Nursery north of town and Mavis Bell lived next door.

"No, not officially, but she still comes down to check on us all the time. She's busy with her new business, but she also has those chickens to corral." Amanda chuckled. "Mr. Salzman goes over there regularly to help her."

Cora Mae frowned. "Hmm, are the chickens misbehaving?"

"This is all new to Mavis. She always wanted to have chickens, but she doesn't have any experience with it. Mr. Salzman had them when he was young, so he's helping her out."

"So, Saucy is a chicken whisperer. Who knew?"

Amanda laughed. "Mavis said he has them all named and teaching them tricks."

Cora Mae rolled her eyes. "He'll never let her have a chicken dinner!"

"Oh, no, but I don't think she plans to do that. She wanted the eggs and wanted them for insect control, but she has a dilemma right now. She got a few hens from Eli Buford and then she bought some chicks. Two of the chicks have turned out to be roosters."

"They don't give eggs." Cora Mae tilted her head and pointed her finger. She didn't know much about farm life, but she had that part figured out.

"True, but the real problem is that they don't play well together. A flock should have only one rooster, if it has any, because two will fight each other. She's got them separated right now, but that's just a temporary solution."

"Did Saucy have a resolution?"

"He agrees that she needs to find another home for one of them, but they don't agree on which rooster to keep!" Amanda laughed. "Apparently, one is more assertive than the other. Saucy says he is the true leader of the flock and should stay."

Cora couldn't resist the details. "And Mavis wants the other one. Why?"

"It's prettier."

Cora Mae shook her head and laughed. "I may have to go out there and check out this chicken farm myself."

"You could be the tie breaker!" Amanda nodded. Mavis had already asked Amanda for her opinion and she wasn't taking sides.

"I barely know one end of a chicken from the other, so I don't think I'm a proper judge. Has she asked your dad?" Amanda's father, Hymie Morgan, was the veterinarian at the Spicetown Animal Clinic.

"She did, and he told her she didn't need a rooster unless she wanted to go into the chick business. If she just wants eggs, he suggested she give both roosters away."

Cora Mae shrugged. She was out of her element on this topic. "I would imagine it might be difficult to find two roosters a new home."

"I'm afraid it usually ends up that they are served up for dinner." Amanda grimaced.

"Ah, I can't imagine Saucy or Mavis want to think about that after they've named them." Cora Mae shuddered.

"No." Amanda shook her head.

"I know I'm going to be sorry for asking this, but what did they name the roosters?"

Amanda smiled. "Hank Williams and Glen Campbell."

Cora Mae swallowed. "Let me guess. Glen is the pretty one?"

Amanda nodded and laughed. "She says the hens love country music."

Cora Mae shook her head. She regretted her insatiable curiosity sometimes.

Chapter 4

"The truck is moving!" Arlene called out to Peggy, who had her head in a box in the back room. She had just gotten a new shipment of yarn and was anxious to see the new colors and textures. Sometimes she thought she only liked to knit because she loved the feel of the twisted strands of fiber.

"Hallelujah!" Peggy said as she walked out waving a skein of wool in mixed earth tones. "The sun can shine again." The truck blocked not only their view across the street, but the sunlight that usually came in the front windows.

"Is that new?" Arlene pointed at the yarn.

"Yes! They've sent some beautiful new colors. You know I love ombres. This is called Autumn Swirl, but they have a jewel-toned collection, too."

"It's very pretty. Can it be used for pooling?"

"It doesn't mention that on the label." Peggy squinted to read the small print. "I can send an email and ask, though."

"Ross Miniken is walking around again. He must make twenty loops a day." Arlene rolled her eyes. She didn't care for the new accountant in town. He had opened an office in the old Hart & Grace Tax Service building just off Fennel Street. "He walks to the community center and crosses the street, only to walk down to Paprika Parkway and crosses again. It's driving me batty!"

Peggy laughed. "You've mentioned that and I'm beginning to think you might be protesting too much." Despite the scowling, Arlene could not stop watching Ross Miniken when he passed by. Peggy had not forgotten Arlene's first impression of the pretentious, but good-looking older man that had recently moved to town and opened business on Clove Street.

Arlene feigned disgust. "I heard he was seen in the bakery having coffee with Miriam Landry last week. They make a fine pair."

"She's probably tempting him with her business and dangling her demands that he join the Chamber of Commerce over his head. She never let Jacob Hart handle her finances. I think she must take them to someone in Paxton."

"Of course not! Jacob helped all of us and she couldn't be seen mingling with commoners." Arlene chuckled.

"That and Jacob probably wasn't a Chamber member. He was a sweetheart of a guy, but not much of a joiner. He really didn't need anything from the Chamber and wouldn't spend his money foolishly."

"I wonder what happened with his building." Arlene looked out the front window, but could only see the corner of the Hart & Grace Tax Service Building. "His son refused to rent to Ross Miniken, so either Ross bought the building, or someone else did."

Peggy shrugged. She had forgotten about that stand-off and didn't know how it had gotten resolved.

"We need to get the knitting group started up again." Arlene walked back to the counter and opened the laptop. "I could send an email to our subscribers that we have a new yarn shipment and they get twenty percent off if they show a copy of their email at time of purchase. What do you think?"

Peggy nodded. "You could do that. We could start the group back the first of September and keep it on Tuesday afternoons. That seemed to work well."

"September?" Arlene scowled.

"You want to start back now?" Peggy smiled. "Most people aren't interested in yarn when it's still eighty degrees outside."

“But I want to know what’s going on in town!” Arlene understood Peggy’s reasoning, but couldn’t help pouting. She had missed attending the group when it had been held at the Keslar Mansion and was excited to bring it back to the store. “I’ll add needlework into the group invite. It can’t hurt to invite everyone. If no one shows at the first few meetings, there is no harm done.”

Peggy laughed. “That’s true. You can give it a try after we get this yarn priced and out on display.” Arlene was right. It would be nice to know what’s going on in town.

Regina waved as the semi-truck pulled away from the curb on Fennel Street with ten minutes to spare. Turning back, she saw Kim, Eden, Heather, and Missy staring at her without a collective thought in their brains, waiting for direction.

“Grab a box, girls. Let’s get it all inside and then we’ll sort everything out.” Kim grabbed the handcart and began stacking boxes on it. Kim was the oldest of the gang, but definitely the most efficient. “Where’s Brook?”

“I think she’s upstairs on the phone.” Heather pointed over her shoulder before leaning down to prop open the door. Missy and Eden each took a box and carried it inside with Regina on their heels.

"Brook? Are you in here?"

Brook walked out from the back room and noticed the truck was no longer blocking their view of the street. "I'm here. What's the plan?"

"We're going to pull the rest inside and sort it out. We need to get the sidewalk clear."

"Gotcha." Brook rushed toward the door.

"Hey, Brook. Were you on the phone? Did Garrett call?" Regina's brother, Garrett, was her financial partner, but he rarely got involved with the onsite setup.

"No. I haven't heard from him."

Regina nodded. Garrett was supposed to call back with details on some deliveries. The custom-made counters were not here yet, and she needed a desk for her office. Customer chairs and break room supplies were coming as well. She couldn't move into the upstairs apartment without a few amenities in place first.

Everyone stepped back as Kim pushed the handcart over the threshold with four boxes stacked high. Regina watched Police Chief Conrad Harris walk by with his police dog without even a sly glance inside. He was probably disappointed he couldn't write her a ticket and tow the truck.

"Let's keep the heavy boxes here and open them first. We may be able to break down the load easier that way." Brook turned around and pointed at Eden, Heather and Missy. "You guys can take those three boxes upstairs. They are all marked as Regina's stuff."

Heather grabbed the lightest box on top and headed for the stairs as Eden and Missy moved slowly behind as if they were uncertain whether they had another flight of stairs in them.

Half way up, Eden leaned over and whispered to Missy. "I'm staying up here unless they make me come down. I'm tired of Brook ordering me around like she's the boss."

Missy smirked. "Well, she is the lead worker on this job."

"Yeah, but she's not staying to take over the store like usual. This isn't her store. Regina is taking this one. She's the real boss."

Missy nodded, but it didn't really matter who gave the orders. The work was the same. She trudged up the stairs as the box dug into her upper arms and focused on the fact tomorrow would be easier. The first couple of days were always the worst.

"Hurry back, girls. I've got an announcement to make." Regina pulled a high stool over and wiggled up onto it to watch Brook and Kim open the larger boxes and wait for the other girls.

"Hurry up, guys," Heather said as she passed Eden and Missy on the stairs going back down. Eden muttered something unintelligible merely for the release and Missy tried to move a little faster.

"What's in there?" Regina pointed to the box Kim and Brook had just opened. The box was marked with the name of one of her distributors but it had been too wide for any one person to get their arms around.

Papers rustled and Kim pushed aside the plastic wrapping before pulling the item out and holding it up. "Short jackets. Some are denim and I think the ones under them are corduroy."

"Fall stuff." Regina nodded. "That's probably all we will get. That's why I wanted to push the grand opening until September. We are in between seasons and everyone is still thinking about how hot they are. I don't want to buy a bunch of summer wear, just to discount it in a month."

Heather jumped off the last step of the stairwell. "I can call around and see if any of the other stores want to ship us some of their overstock. We could ask Missy if her store has excess summer and if we get a little from each store, we could open with summer options."

Missy ran the store in Rochester now but had been pulled away for a few weeks by Regina, when Regina needed an extra hand with this new location.

"That's an excellent idea!" Regina said to Heather and then pointed at Brook. "Tomorrow morning, you need to make some phone calls and see what's available.

We can store the fall merchandise in the back until September and not delay our opening."

Heather opened her mouth to object, but slowly shut it. It had been her idea, but mentioning that was probably not going to be viewed as helpful. She just hoped Regina remembered it.

"Okay, we're back." Missy's chest heaved as she took a deep breath, hoping the big announcement did not involve the stairs. Eden's footsteps stomped on each step as she followed her to the first floor.

"I have two surprises!" Regina clapped her hands together. "The first surprise is..." Regina looked around the room at expectant faces and laughed at all the different reactions. Missy's eyes were wide with wonder and Heather had a curious sparkle of mischief in her smile. That was just what Regina had hoped for. Brook sported a knowing smile because she knew what was coming. Kim's expression was nonplussed. Kim always managed whatever came her way with little emotion, but Eden looked completely horrified by the unknown.

"The first surprise is tomorrow's lunch. I'd like to have a party lunch with everyone bringing a little something different to share. Now I know you can't really cook in your current living arrangements, but it's okay to bring something ready-made. It can be snacks, desserts, salad, vegetables or bread. The only requirement is that it be edible and whatever significant food group is lacking, I will make up the difference! What do you say? Does that sound like fun?"

There was a quiet moment and Regina craned her neck forward to encourage a response. Missy looked around at the others and finally decided to speak after a cleansing breathe. "Yeah, that sounds like fun!"

Kim nodded her head and Brook smiled. "It will be great. We can eat all day while we unpack."

"And now for the second surprise. I'm going to let everyone off early today so they can go shopping and get ready for tomorrow!"

With that news, everyone smiled, even Eden.

Chapter 5

Cora Mae Bingham walked into the Ole Thyme Italian Restaurant and saw strangers sitting in her usual booth. Joann Biglioni approached her as she looked around the room for Conrad Harris.

"Good evening, Mayor. Are you looking for someone?" Joann smiled and resisted the urge to tease Cora Mae about her date. She had seated a stranger at a table who said they were here to dine with the mayor.

"Hi, Joann. Yes, I'm looking for a gentleman named Mr. Abbott. I expect the chief will also join us. Are either of them here?"

"There is a gentleman here that said he was expecting you." Joann's shoulders dropped in disappointment. "I haven't seen the chief yet, though. I'm sorry your booth was taken. I wasn't expecting you tonight."

"A table is better for three. I appreciate it. Where is he?"

Joann pointed to the far front corner and then saw Conrad push open the front door. "The chief is here."

Cora motioned for Conrad to follow her as she wove through the tables and greeted those she knew. Conrad had been briefed by phone that Mr. Abbott was in town and wanted a tour of the community center and more details on available security.

"Good evening, Mr. Abbott. I'm Cora Bingham and this is Police Chief Harris."

Conrad pulled a chair out for Cora Mae and then shook Mr. Abbott's hand. "Nice to meet you. The Stromboli is on special tonight and I highly recommend it."

Joann showed up at the table just as introductions were concluding. The visitor had been looking at the menu for over ten minutes, so he should have formed a plan by now and she knew what Cora and Conrad wanted. They were frequent visitors to the Ole Thyme Italian and creatures of habit.

After orders were taken and drinks provided, Cora Mae turned to Mr. Abbott. "Did you receive the information I emailed to you this afternoon? I know you were probably on the road, but I did send you some details on our insurance coverage for the community center and a basic floor plan."

"I have glanced at it on my phone, but I'll need to take a thorough look tomorrow once I have my laptop available."

"Mayor Bingham mentioned you have some security concerns?" Conrad sat back in his chair and tilted his head. Overtime had frequently been used to cover town events but there was a limited budget for that. Conrad couldn't imagine train sets would bring thieves out of the woodwork.

"I do. We have had circumstances in the past that have made me cautious of theft and destruction. These exhibits are not toys, and although we cannot prohibit children from attending, parents have been lax in their responsibilities when it comes to controlling their children in public." Mr. Abbott cringed when a child in the restaurant squealed loudly in protest at a nearby table. "I have been forced to require acrylic barriers be in place at all exhibits, but that has not completely remedied the problem."

"As I mentioned on the telephone, we do have the barriers we can put into place to prevent the public from handling your exhibits. When you mentioned security to me over the phone, I was under the impression you were concerned about theft. I apologize for the misunderstanding. A police presence will not be effective for children's mischief. What other suggestions do you have?"

"You did not misunderstand. There are just two issues at play. To secure the exhibit, we need a barrier from the floor up to prevent visitors from reaching around or crawling under. Hanging acrylic or using stanchions to rope off the walkway have not been sufficient in the past.

"In addition, a police presence is required. We have suffered loss from prior showings and although the exhibit travels with a security detail, they will require assistance."

Conrad cleared his throat. "There's an exhibit in Pittsburgh that is open to the public. I'm assuming your displays are similar to those, but they don't put up barriers on them. They're on large tables and the trains move among the little villages they have created. Is that what you are setting up?"

Cora Mae's side-eyed glance at Conrad registered surprise.

"That is a government sponsored display that is designed for entertainment. This is a private exhibit of collectors' items that are difficult or impossible to replace." Mr. Abbott's haughty sneer was showing through.

"I assume then, that you have this collection highly insured." Cora glanced at Conrad, wondering why Mr. Abbott cared about the insurance coverage at the community center. He should be carrying his own policy.

"We do, yes, but one cannot put a price on something which cannot be replaced."

But obviously one does, Conrad thought, as he remained expressionless, pining away for his Stromboli. "This is a Saturday and Sunday afternoon only, right?" Conrad turned to Cora for confirmation. "No night viewing hours."

"That's correct," Mr. Abbott said. "Although the collection will remain in the community center overnight on Saturday."

Conrad nodded and quickly calculated overtime pay in his head. "I can give you two uniforms for the Saturday viewing hours and one on Sunday afternoon."

"And what protection is available outside of those hours?" Mr. Abbott's chin rose as Cora's mouth opened.

Conrad rushed to speak before Cora promised his overtime allotment away. "Regular patrol is available around the clock. The community center is included in our regular patrol path."

"The community center has a state-of-the-art security system. It doesn't require an armed sentry." Cora Mae was getting miffed and her attempts to disguise it with earnest concern were dissolving. Conrad tapped the side of Cora's foot with his own.

"You said you were bringing a security detail with you. Are they staying with the collection at night?"

Conrad relaxed when Cora Mae leaned back in her chair with a calm resolve. "I will need to make certain my officers are aware of their presence, if they do plan to stay on site."

"They have not stayed in the past. That is something I would have to discuss with them. It would likely cause me to incur additional expense, which would require our fee to increase."

Cora leaned back in her chair as Joann approached with their orders on a large tray. Silence fell across the table until everyone's meal was correctly placed in front of them, and Joann walked away.

Cora pulled her cloth napkin free from her utensils and shook it out to drape over her lap. "Perhaps Spicetown is just not a good fit for your collection, Mr. Abbott."

Arlene Emery walked through the front door of the Ole Thyme Italian Restaurant and gave a small wave to Christine Gossett when she caught her eye. Christine smiled and walked over once she finished taking the order of a couple sitting in the corner booth.

"Hi, Mrs. Emery." Christine reached for menus. "Are you ready for a table?"

"Yes, dear. I'm expecting Peggy Cochran to show up soon, so there will just be two of us."

"Follow me."

Arlene waved at Cora as they passed her table to walk toward the back and then she slid into the booth.

Arlene leaned forward and lowered her voice. "Who's the guy with the mayor? Do you know him?"

Christine looked over her shoulder and turned back to place menus on the table. "No. I've never seen him before."

"Hmm, okay. Thanks." Arlene scrunched up her face to avoid pouting again. *This town was going crazy with new people and she couldn't keep up!*

Watching the front door, hoping to catch Peggy's eye if she walked in, Arlene saw the doors swing open. *Ross Miniken! Why does he keep showing up everywhere?* Arlene grabbed a menu, opened it wide and held it up to cover her face. *He better not come this way.*

Peeking around the menu, she saw him in deep discussion with Joann Biglioni as they both looked around the restaurant and pointed. Suddenly, Joann grabbed an empty chair, entirely too close to Arlene's booth and moved it away from the table as Ross grabbed the edge of the table to drag it even closer to her. It was clear they were arranging for a large group to sit right next to her booth! She was trapped.

Peggy pulled her truck into a parking place and

watched as Regina Adkins walked down the sidewalk and up the side ramp to the Ole Thyme Italian Restaurant. Her first instinct was to call Arlene and abort this mission, but Arlene hadn't needed to carry an overweight English bulldog home first, so she was most likely already sitting inside waiting on her. She wished now she hadn't seen the sign about Stromboli being the special tonight.

Marching up the ramp incline behind Regina was a line of her loyal workers following like ducks in a row. Dinner was ruined.

Chapter 6

"Wow, what a collection we have!" Regina beamed as she looked over all the dishes on the table the next morning. "You all did a wonderful job."

"Do we have to wait until lunch time?" Heather sniffed the air.

"I brought pastries from the bakery next door, so we have to eat those now while they're warm!" Kim opened a white box filled with an assortment of scones, turnovers, and donuts. "This can be the morning food and we'll have the pie for afternoon break."

Regina shook her head. "We may not get much done today after all."

Brook reached for a donut and thanked Kim. "I brought a chocolate meringue pie because that's my favorite and I couldn't resist it when I saw it in the display case. I hope everyone likes chocolate!"

"Of course," Missy said as she arranged the chips and dip at one end of the counter.

"You said you made arrangements for the refrigeration, right?" Brook picked up her pie. "I need to keep this cool."

"Yes, I'm going to take my meat tray, your pie, and the cheesecake across the street. The girls at the craft shop have a fridge we can use." Regina pointed at the cheesecake, and Heather handed it across the table.

"I can take that over for you." Kim stacked the pies on top of the tray. They each had a plastic lid to protect them. "I'll need someone to grab the door for me."

As Missy pulled open the door, Ross Miniken stepped back in surprise. "Well, good morning!" Seeing Kim stagger back with a wobbling step, he reached out to grab the two pie plates. "Let me help."

Kim sighed. "I'm taking them across the street to put in the refrigerator."

"I'll tag along." Ross waved at Regina. "I'm going to go with Kim. We'll be right back."

Regina nodded and opened a bag of chips. "I know it's early, but I need something salty now that I've had something sweet."

"Me, too!" Eden held her hand out for the bag after Regina poured some on a plate.

"Thank you for catching those pies." Kim ducked

her head shyly. "I was afraid I was going to lose them."

"Glad I was at the right place at the right time. Are we going in the craft shop?"

"Yes. Regina talked to them yesterday and they said they had a little room. The restaurants said they weren't allowed to keep anything like that with their own food because it was against the law."

Ross frowned. That sounded like malarkey. "This is handy, and you don't have too much to store. You girls all have refrigerators in the places you are renting, don't you? I know some of you are living without much furniture."

"I do. I actually have a nice place. It's smaller than the other girls, but there is some furniture still there. I think mine is a rental and their places are on the market for sale. Did you buy a home here yet? Regina mentioned you were looking." Kim looked both ways before she stepped out onto Fennel Street to cross.

"Not yet. I'm still staying at the Nutmeg Inn. I'm going to look at a few houses this afternoon, but I'm really not very good at house shopping. My wife always took the lead in those things and I just adjusted to whatever she chose. Everything Clyde shows me seems okay, but nothing feels like home."

Kim nodded and reached for the door handle.

Peggy looked over when she heard the door open

and saw Kim with a wide smile, carrying a large round tray. It was an awkward size, but at least it was just one item. Peggy had expected Regina to take advantage of their hospitality.

"Hi, Kim. You must need the refrigerator." Peggy smiled and waved her in. Kim was the only worker Regina had that seemed to have any manners. She was always cordial and polite when she visited the craft store, but she also did a little sewing when she had the time. Sadly, her current job kept her traveling and she hadn't been able to use her free time well, but she did buy a small cross stitch kit to try it.

"Hi, Peggy. I have two pies with this, but they can sit on top. Do you think you'll have room?"

Peggy saw that Ross Miniken was coming in the door behind Kim with the pies. Arlene was next door in the shipping store and she hoped she could get him out of the building before Arlene came back. After last night, Arlene did not need another run-in with him.

"Let's go see. Follow me."

Arlene walked around the shipping counter and stood in the arched doorway to the craft store just as Ross Miniken followed Kim into the back room. She didn't see his face, but she knew the back of his head well now, after having it in front of her face all evening at the restaurant. He must be bringing over the food for the

Sassafras luncheon.

Last night, it looked as though he had invited Regina and all of her employees out to dinner. They had moved two tables together and all dined as a group right near her booth. Ross and Regina couldn't have known each other before moving to Spicetown, but it appeared Ross was very much engaged in getting to know each of the girls better. Just when she thought he was showing a special interest in one, he would move to the next. Most of the girls were half his age and none of them were moving here, but he seemed happy living in this fantasy realm. Arlene found the idea revolting.

"Good morning, Mrs. Emery." Ross bowed his head in greeting when he emerged from the back room.

"Good morning, Mr. Miniken."

"Hey, Arlene." Kim walked around Ross and stepped in front of him. "I'm almost done with the butterflies. I've got them in my purse, but I'll try to remember to bring them over to show you. They don't look as smooth as yours, though, but I like the stitching. I think next time I want something without so many different colors. I hate changing colors."

Arlene laughed. "I know the perfect thing! They have black and red patterns where you never change color."

"That sounds great! Do you have any on display?"

"No, not right now, but I can show you some

pictures when you have time." Arlene wanted her to take Ross out of the store right now and come back later without her shadow. "I know it sounds dull, but the simplicity is actually quite beautiful and it has a vintage feel. I made a very pretty Christmas wreath in red and also a rooster for my sister-in-law once. You can do them as embroidery or cross stitch, but they would be easier for beginners."

"That's me! I'm game. I'll stop back by when I can. Thanks." Kim walked to the door and looked back over her shoulder for Ross.

"Thank you both for the use of your refrigerator." Ross nodded his head once at Peggy and then turned to repeat the action toward Arlene.

Enough with the bowing! Arlene struggled not to roll her eyes, but looked at Peggy instead.

"You're welcome." Peggy walked back to the fabric she had been pricing and waved goodbye to Kim. Ross followed her out quietly.

"Ugh!" Arlene shuddered. "I can't believe she brought him over here with her."

Peggy chuckled. "You are going to have to get a grip on this thing. He is opening a business half a block away and he's going to be living in this town. I admit, I find him a little odd and off-putting, but he's polite. I think he's trying to fit in."

"He does seem interested in companionship. I'll

admit that." Arlene sneered. "He's trying to fit in with every woman he sees."

Peggy sat back and looked at Arlene. "What started all this?"

"All what?"

"This Ross Miniken loathing you have. It's not like you at all. I know you found him a bit pretentious when you first met on the street that day, but your contempt has grown since then. Have you had other conversations with him that you haven't told me about?"

"I run into him every time I turn around! He's positively unavoidable!"

Peggy shook her head. "But have you talked to him? Has he said something more to offend you?"

"He doesn't engage with me unless he has to, but I've overheard many things he's said. He continues to denigrate Spicetown and everyone in it. I don't know what to do about it, but I cannot hardly look at him."

"Is this rumor or something you heard yourself?" Peggy gave Arlene a warning sideways glance. This town could whip up a dust storm over nothing if it involved an outsider.

"No, I heard it myself. Last month he showed up at my church on Sunday morning. He was very nice at first, almost too nice. I felt like he was trying too hard to flatter me and it made me uncomfortable, but I was pleasant to him."

“So, what happened?” Peggy put the pricing gun down to give Arlene her full attention.

“I showed him where the Sunday School rooms were for the adults and gave him a short tour. It was all very polite, but then later I heard him talking to Donna LeMasters. It was as if he rewound our conversation on a tape and played it again. She responded better than I did.” Arlene shrugged. “Donna was gushing all over him when he tried drowning her in flattery. She was eating it up. I was a bit embarrassed for her, but anyway, then he told her that he didn’t want to go to the classroom he’d been shown. He said her class looked like more his style.”

Peggy’s eyes darted around the room when Arlene paused. “And you think that was an attack on you?”

“Yes!” Arlene scowled. “He’s trying to act like he’s half his age and flirting with every woman he meets.”

“Okay, so he’s a player. I can see why you don’t want to get into a conversation where he’s going to start imitating Casanova, but I still don’t see why you can’t keep him at a polite distance. You can be civil...”

“I’m not done.” Arlene held up her hand. “After Sunday School class ended, we were milling about in the hallway and working our way toward the auditorium, when he ran into Clyde Newman. He asked Clyde about a house that Red Pepper Realty just listed and they made arrangements for him to see it. He told Clyde then that this town had nothing of interest to offer him and he was concerned he had made a mistake coming here.

"Clyde told him that he had found him a business location and they would find a suitable home, but Ross said he didn't even know places like this existed." Arlene shuddered again.

"So, he sounds frustrated. Cut him some slack."

"I have!" Arlene glared at Peggy. "I didn't kick him in the shins that morning, but I wanted to!"

Peggy laughed and picked up her pricing gun. "Thata girl! Give it time. He'll come around." Everyone didn't want the same thing in a home or a hometown.

Arlene gave Peggy a sinister side glance. "Or he'll wish he had."

Chapter 7

Cora Mae waved Conrad Harris into her office and took off her reading glasses to rub her tired eyes. Conrad had Briscoe's leash in one hand and a large brown bag in the other.

"Where do you want this?" Conrad held the bag up over Cora's desk, but she waved him toward the conference table.

"Let's eat over there." Cora stood up slowly and slipped her feet back into her shoes. She needed to stand up and stretch.

Conrad dropped the bag on the table and then walked Briscoe over to the corner of the room so he could relax while they had lunch. "Bad day so far?"

"Not much success." Cora pulled a chair out to sit as Conrad pulled dinner containers out of the bag from the cafe. "The railroad show is not going to happen. I've finally admitted defeat and it's time to move on."

"You couldn't find anyone else?" Conrad passed Cora a napkin.

"There are several traveling shows, but they need more room than we have in our community center and they're much more expensive. I couldn't find anyone else that traveled with a smaller private collection."

"I think the guy would have been trouble anyway. Something didn't feel right about the whole thing. His demands weren't reasonable, and the toy train isn't carrying the Hope diamond! It doesn't need armed guards around the clock."

Cora Mae chuckled and wrinkled her nose. "I wonder if other towns actually provide that to him. I almost think he wanted us to cancel and he kept imposing more demands to see what it would take."

"Well, I'm glad you threw in the towel on that one."

"Saucy won't be, though, and I feel bad about that. I'll have to find some way to make it up to him. Oh, I didn't get a chance last night to ask you about Georgia. How is the Georgia and Roy switch going so far?"

Conrad wiped his mouth and smiled. "A little sideways. Georgie is great! No problems at all. She hit the street like she never left."

"And Roy?"

"He can answer the phone when it rings." Conrad

laughed. "But he has not mastered the radio."

"Oh, dear. Aren't the other officers suffering?"

"They're giving Roy a hard time, but I was counting on that. After a few weeks of this, his days of disrespecting Georgia should end. He needs to learn to appreciate her a little more and everyone else knows that, too. They'll all get by until my little experiment is over, but I'm not letting him off that assignment until he learns the job."

"Sometimes everyone must suffer for the greater good." Cora Mae smiled. Roy Asher was a frustration to Conrad, but she wasn't convinced yet he could be much more than that.

After eating quietly for a few minutes, Cora Mae heard voices in Amanda's outer office and Conrad's head turned when he heard the muffled sound. "Is that Saucy?"

"Could be." Cora pushed back her chair and walked to her doorway.

"Oh, I'm sorry, Mayor. I didn't mean to disturb you." Saucy held his hands up in alarm. "I just had a question."

Cora looked at Amanda, who shrugged helplessly. "Come on in. We're just having a bite to eat." Cora walked back to her seat at the table with Saucy creeping behind.

"I'm sorry, Chief. I really didn't mean to interrupt

anyone's lunch. I was just at the counter out front and had a question about something the young lady told me."

"Well, have a seat." Conrad pointed to a chair and returned to his meal.

Saucy glanced in the corner of the room when he saw Briscoe's ear twitch and declined the chair Conrad offered. He was fascinated with the Chief's police dog when it was restrained at a distance, but terrified of him when he was near. "No, thank you. I just have one simple question."

"Okay." Cora turned her attention to Saucy and waited for the miracle to happen. There was nothing simple about Harvey Salzman.

"What do I need to do to change a city ordinance?"

"Well, you can't actually change it, but you can try to convince the city council to enact a new ordinance to replace it. It doesn't happen overnight though. It takes some time."

"Okay, so how do I convince them? Do I need to get on the agenda for the next meeting? And what do you mean by time? Is it days or months or years?"

Cora Mae shook her head. One question had turned into many, just as she expected. "There are different ways to go about changing public opinion. You can write a letter to the Spicetown Star editor. You can get a petition signed by a few hundred citizens. You can hold a public hearing and invite the town. It all depends on whether you can find other people that feel the same way you do. There's strength in numbers. What exactly is it you want to change, Saucy?"

Saucy frowned and mumbled through his confusion. "I asked Ms. Laura out front if I could keep a rooster at my house and she said no. She said there is an ordinance that says only hens are allowed in city limits."

"Laura is correct. Do you have chickens now?" Cora's brow furrowed as she braced herself for the answer. Mavis' chicken farm may have just spilled over to Dill Seed Drive.

"No, ma'am, and I don't plan to get chickens. I just want to keep a rooster, and I don't see why that should be a problem to the town. It's just one bird. Everybody else gets to have a pet. They can even have a bird in a cage, so why can't I have just one rooster?"

Conrad paused between bites and turned in his chair to offer his contribution. "Because you can't sneak the sunrise past a rooster and your neighbors will want to suffocate you while you sleep!"

Cora Mae held her hand close to her mouth to hide her smile.

"But he's not that loud and there aren't any houses behind me. Mrs. Greer next door doesn't hear well. She probably won't even notice."

Cora planted her elbow on the table and dropped her chin into the palm of her hand. "Saucy, is this about

Glen Campbell?"

Saucy's eyes doubled in size and Conrad's head lifted as the pickle fell out of his sandwich. "Glen Campbell?"

"Have you met him?" Saucy began wringing his hands. "He's a really good boy, and Hank Williams is beating him up every day. He needs a safe place to stay. I don't want either of them to get hurt."

"Wait." Conrad dabbed a napkin across his chin. "I've missed a chunk of this story somewhere."

Cora Mae smiled. "Yes, I know about Mavis' problem with the two roosters, but I don't think the answer is changing a city ordinance. I don't think the citizens or the council would support it."

"I don't know what else to do. I don't really want to move out of town." Saucy pouted. "I like being able to walk downtown when the weather is nice."

"Oh, Saucy! You don't need to move. You just need to find Hank and Glen a new home. There are plenty of people living around the area that have the space to take in a rooster, and you know everybody. You might even talk to Shelby Worth at the animal shelter. She knows all the animal lovers in the area and she's had chickens dropped off there before. I'm sure she found them a home.

"You just need to think a little more on this before you go trying to change city ordinances."

Saucy nodded. "Maybe you're right, Mayor. I'll go think on this some more."

Just as Saucy turned to go with his head hanging low, Conrad called out. "Herman Latley."

Saucy looked back over his shoulder with a spark in his eye. "I know Herman."

"Herman's mom raises dozens of chickens and sells the eggs in Red River at the farmer's market. Herman may have some himself, but either way, I think he can help."

"Thank you, Chief! That's a great idea. I'll go see if I can find him right now. Thank you!"

Cora Mae sighed before returning to her lunch. During that one simple question, Conrad had finished his.

Chapter 8

"Let's clear off this table, so we can get back to work. We didn't get hardly anything done yesterday." Regina glared at Heather who was sticking her hand in a bag of corn chips left over from their luncheon the day before. "Except eating."

Kim smiled at no one in particular. She had enjoyed the snacks, but Heather jerked her hand from the chip bag and sneered at her. Kim shook her head in bewilderment when she saw Heather recoil and walk away from the table. She hadn't meant anything by it and didn't want to be in the middle of anything.

"I wasn't the only one eating. I think everyone had their share." Heather's brief embarrassment at being called out by Regina was turning to rage. She struggled with her weight and didn't appreciate it when she was singled out for it.

"We all ate until we were stuffed. It was a lot of fun, but the faster we get this done, the sooner you can all get back to your family and friends. Let's get busy." Regina clapped her hands. "Let's break down those boxes and then we need to move all of our boxes away from this wall. I've got a handyman coming today to hang some shelves for us and he'll need room on that side."

"Who is the handyman? Is he cute?" Heather shrugged innocently, trying to bat her eyes.

Regina hesitated and decided not to scold. "I haven't met him yet, but his name is Herman. Herman and Heather, it has a nice ring to it." Regina laughed when Heather's face winced in disappointment.

Kim picked up a box labeled for Regina's room. "I'm going to take this upstairs. There's still one more, but I'll come back for it."

"Okay. Thank you. If you see Brook up there, send her down. Eden, I need this box unpacked in the back room. You can stack these on the shelves by the desk."

Eden nodded and took the box of merchandise.

"Missy, you can push this to the back room, too. It's all winter coats and they need to come out of the boxes and up on a rack back there." The box was too wide to get her arms around, so Missy slid it over the tiled flooring as Eden jumped out of the way.

Kim returned for the second box and hollered out

to Regina. "I didn't see Brook upstairs."

Regina frowned. "Where is she? She's supposed to be calling the other stores about excess summer merchandise. Has anyone seen her?" Walking into the storeroom, she peered around the boxes and asked Eden and Missy, but no one had seen her. Grabbing her phone from her back pocket, she dialed Brook's number but it rang without an answer.

"Has anyone seen Brook at all today?" Regina yelled out, pivoting her head from side to side to ensure an individual response from each one. "Anyone?" When no one could confirm a sighting, Regina sighed. The handyman would be arriving soon and she couldn't leave right now. The one morning when Ross Miniken could actually be helpful, he hadn't stopped in. She considered calling him, but she couldn't remember the house number for Brook's rental, anyway.

"Who wants to run over there and bang on her door? I can't leave right now." She'd had employees sleep in before, but Brook was usually very responsible.

"I'll go." Heather nodded and went to grab her purse. "Do you need anything else while I'm out?"

"No, I don't think so. Call me if there's going to be a delay." Regina watched Heather as she walked towards the door and then chuckled. "I'd hate for you to miss Herman!"

Heather rolled her eyes dramatically and laughed,

glad the mood had lifted. "Be right back!"

Arlene crossed and uncrossed her legs, trying to keep her attention on the magazine in her lap that was over a year old, waiting for the receptionist to call her name. Her lab results were back and the new doctor wanted to talk to her. She wasn't really frightened, because she felt fine, but she did have some trepidation that the doctor had found something to discuss at all. That sounded like the beginning of the end, the beginning of a slow ride downhill to death.

Arlene's mother had died from cancer that began from a simple doctor visit for what she thought was indigestion. Her father had known his heart was bad but refused to let it change the way he lived the remainder of his life. Arlene was not like either of them. She made deliberate decisions toward maintaining her health and regularly sought care for preventative measures. Surely, if they'd found something, it would be early enough to treat.

Arlene tensed when the nurse opened the side door and filled her lungs with air preparing to launch from her seat at the sound of her name.

"Randy?"

A young man rose from his chair and followed the nurse through the door, just as the front door opened.

Arlene sighed and felt the tension unravel as she returned to her magazine.

The glass window slid open and the receptionist's muffled conversation began.

"Ross Miniken."

Arlene froze and kept her eyes on the page of summer picnic recipes as if she had every intention of making that raspberry rhubarb pie.

"Just have a seat." The glass partition slid shut and Arlene saw legs walk by her, but she did not look up. She began to read the detailed steps required to prepare the pie filling, hoping he kept walking to the other side of the room.

"Good morning, Mrs. Emery! How are you today?"

Arlene's head turned to the side for a moment before returning to her recipe. "I'm fine. Thank you."

"Well, I'm glad to hear that. Sometimes these places gather people together for unfortunate reasons, so I'm glad to hear that you are doing well."

Arlene nodded without looking up, murmuring a weak thank you, and returning her focus to her magazine. She couldn't bring herself to talk to him or even look at him, and Peggy was right. This was not like her at all. The polite response would have been to ask about his health, but she just couldn't do it. She had always had the ability to be pleasant and welcoming to everyone, friend or foe, but Ross Miniken triggered a protective force field that blocked her natural response from coming through.

The side door opened again and a different nurse said, "Arlene?"

Snapping the magazine closed, Arlene bolted from her chair and greeted the nurse warmly, feeling relief that her true personality was still in there.

"Follow me. We're going to put you right here in the second room on your left. You can put your purse in the chair and have a seat. The doctor will be with you in just a moment."

Arlene thanked her and relaxed in her safe hiding place. She had escaped Ross Miniken again, but how long would this go on? He kept showing up everywhere she went and she would need to resolve this anxiety. Maybe she needed therapy?

"Good morning, Mrs. Emery." Dr. Julie Sachs walked into the exam room door with her laptop open and pushed the door shut with her toe as she tried to read the screen. "It looks like you are just here today for lab results. Let's take a look."

Arlene nodded and waited quietly as the doctor plugged her laptop into a docking station and took a seat.

"Are you feeling okay? Do you have any concerns

today?"

"I'm fine." She started to ask if she should have concerns and then thought better of it.

"Well, your results show a couple of things that I think we can address easy enough. Your Vitamin D is very low, too low, and we need to bring that up. It's very common in the later years. I see a lot of women your age with Vitamin D deficiencies and that's why I test for it. We'll give you a mega-dose by prescription to get you where you need to be and then you can take a drugstore supplement daily to keep your levels where they need to be."

"Okay." Arlene took a deep relaxing breath. That was painless.

"I think it will actually make you feel better once we make that adjustment. Low Vitamin D can make you feel fatigued or depressed, but it's such a gradual thing that most people don't notice it or they think it's just age related. We can fix that!"

"Okay. That sounds easy."

"Yes, it is. The other result I was concerned about was your iron. It's very low as well. This is another deficit that can bring on fatigue. Do you eat meat?"

"Yes, but not every day."

"There are other foods rich in iron. Seafood, beans, and green vegetables are a good source of iron, but I'd like to get your levels up with a supplement, and then maybe with some diet changes you will be able to maintain that. We'll recheck your labs in six months and see how it looks then. Does that sound okay?"

"Yes!" Arlene hoped that was all she found and Dr. Sachs wasn't saving her prediction of imminent death for last.

"Good! Your record says Chervil Drugs. Is that where you want them sent?"

"Yes."

"We'll get those both called in for you today, and you let me know if you have any problems with them. Okay?"

"Yes, that will be great. Thank you, Dr. Sachs. I appreciate it."

Arlene grabbed her purse and the nurse came to the door to point her to the checkout. Relieved at her results and prompt service she plopped her purse on the counter to pay, just as panic squeezed her heart. The appointment went so quickly, Ross Miniken may still be sitting out there waiting for his name to be called and she would have to face yet another encounter with the man she wanted most to avoid.

Chapter 9

"She's not coming to the door." Heather huffed into the phone. She had already tried ringing the doorbell, banging on the door, and walking around to the back to see if there was a way to see inside. "I've made all kinds of racket and nothing. What do you want me to do?"

Creases formed between Regina's eyebrows as she pondered her options. "Let me call Clyde Newman. He would have a key. Stand by." Regina hung up on Heather and tapped Clyde's phone number in her recent call history, but the call went to voice mail.

"Clyde, this is Regina Atkins. If you get this message in the next few minutes, would you please drive by that rental you set up for me on Lemon Lane? One of my girls is over there and can't get in. Thank you."

She thought about calling the police for a well

check, but the chief was already so irritated with her she was afraid he might feel she was overstepping. Clyde could be tied up for an hour if he was showing houses today or setting up a new listing, but she felt like she needed to give him a chance before she went over there and broke into the house. Plus, she was still waiting for the handyman.

"Ross!" Regina threw her hands up in the air when he walked into the store. "You have perfect timing. I could really use a favor from you."

"Sure. How can I help?" Looking around the room that was in a disorderly mess, he hoped it did not involve straightening up.

"One of my girls didn't get up this morning and Heather is over there trying to get her to come to the door. I left a message with Clyde Newman to come with a key, but I don't know when he'll be free to help. Would you mind going over there to see if you can help her? I'm waiting for the handyman to show up and I need to be here when he arrives."

"Not at all. I can run over there. Where is it?"

"On Lemon Lane, uh." Regina looked around at the other girls for help. "It's a little gray house a couple of blocks north of the library. I don't know the house number, but Heather is there now. I'll tell her to stay by her car so you can see her."

Ross nodded and pulled open the door. "I'll be right

back."

Regina sent Heather a text that Ross was coming to help and then noticed everyone was just staring at her, rather than working. "Let's get busy. We're two people down now. Missy, come help me with these cabinet doors. They just slide into the hinges but you have to line up the top and bottom just right. I need you to hold them so I can guide them in."

Ross found Heather's car easily as she was parked on the street and sitting in the driver's seat with the door wide open blocking traffic, so he pulled in behind her. As he walked up, she was flipping through her phone and looking at videos, but glanced up at him and smiled.

"I've tried everything and she's not answering. You can try it though if you want."

"Who is staying here? Regina didn't even tell me."

"Oh, it's Brook. Do you know her? She's the young one with the dark hair. She's Regina's right hand for this opening. She always picks someone to be lead."

"Is she that sound a sleeper?" Ross was concerned the girl was unconscious, but everyone else seemed calm about her not responding to the doorbell.

"I have no idea. I mean, I don't know her that well, but she's usually on time for work." Heather shut her car door and followed Ross to the porch. "I can hear the doorbell ringing so I know it's not broken."

"What about around back? Is there a sliding glass door or anything you can see in?"

"There's a glass door, but the curtain is pulled shut."

Ross frowned, but had to go through the motions of ringing the bell a dozen times and banging his fist on the door without result. Looking across the street, he became concerned there might be curious onlookers. This town seemed to have a tight network of citizens that had a natural distrust of outsiders. He wouldn't be surprised to see the police show up from a neighbor reporting unusual activity.

"Did you notice whether the sliding glass door had a rod in the sliding track?"

Heather's forehead furrowed. "What do you mean?"

"The metal track at the bottom." Ross pointed to the base of the front door. "The place where the door slides. Did you see a broom handle or metal bar on the track? People put them in there to keep someone from breaking in."

"Uh, I didn't look. I didn't notice one, but I wasn't looking for it either."

"If there isn't one, we can probably get inside. Let me get a screwdriver from my car." Ross opened the back door of his sedan and looked around in a small bag he kept behind the seat until he found a large flathead screwdriver. "Let's go around back."

Heather followed him, excited about the prospect of breaking into the house, but finally beginning to wonder what they'd find.

Ross looked down and pointed at the track on the stationary side of the window. "See the track. That's where you should always put a metal bar or broom handle to keep people from breaking into your house." Ross placed the edge of the screwdriver under the bottom of the door near the opening and reached up to grab the handle. Pushing down on the screwdriver to raise the door up while pulling back on the handle at the same time, the door sprang open.

"Wow!"

"Remember that if you ever buy a house with a sliding door." Ross pointed the screwdriver at Heather.

Heather smiled and nodded her head.

"Let's look carefully. I don't want to scare her to death." Ross pushed the curtain back as Heather followed him inside. "Brook! Brook, are you here?"

"Brook. Brook, wake up!" Heather turned right toward the living room because Ross had gone left toward the kitchen. She wasn't sure where the bedrooms were, but she kept calling her name.

Ross saw her first. The young girl was on the kitchen floor. Falling to his knees beside her he put his hand on her neck, but she was cold to the touch and her muscles tense. Pulling his phone from his pocket, he dialed 9-1-1 just as Heather came through the kitchen door and screamed.

Arlene looked out the front window of the Carom Seed Craft Corner again. She had seen Ross go in briefly and leave earlier, but now Saucy was on the sidewalk.

"Is he back again?" Peggy asked when she saw Arlene peering out the window. She had heard the story of the doctor visit and was still perplexed at Arlene's reaction to Ross Miniken, but she didn't know how to help her get past it.

"No, Saucy is out there. He's in an animated conversation with Herman Latley on the sidewalk in front of Sassafras. I don't know what they could be talking about, but it's clear that Saucy is wound up about it."

"I gave Herman's name to Regina a couple of days ago. She was looking for someone to help her put up some shelving. I told her he might be free to help her and he doesn't charge an arm and a leg. I think he's working part-time for the city now though, so you have to catch him on his day off."

Arlene chuckled watching Saucy's arms flail in demonstrative explanation. "Herman seems calm, so whatever Saucy is stressed about isn't affecting him. He does have his toolbox with him, so you're probably right. It looks like he's talking about somebody fighting or getting attacked. He's acting it all out."

The show drew Peggy to the window and they both laughed when Saucy began to flap his elbows like he was going to fly away. "You should have taken a video of this! This is hilarious. Even Herman is chuckling now."

Just as Saucy seemed to conclude his story, his face lit up with a smile. He shook Herman's hand and patted his arm. Herman nodded and smiled although Saucy's diatribe continued until the door to Sassafras flew open and Regina came flying out in a panic.

"Now what's going on?" Peggy frowned. "She's not coming over here, is she?"

"No, I think her car is parked on this side of the road. She has a crazy look in her eye." Arlene stood on her tiptoes to see around the corner. "Yeah, she just jumped in her car."

"Oh, look. Kim's outside now talking to Herman and Saucy. I wonder what's going on."

"Saucy has the most expressive face. He looks like he's in shock now."

Arlene waved when Saucy turned to look their way.

"Herman's going inside with Kim. Maybe Saucy will come over here and tell us what's going on."

Chapter 10

"Spicetown Police. How can I help you?" Roy Asher slipped half of his cheese stick under the desk and Briscoe snapped it up.

"This is Ross Miniken and I'm calling to report I've found a dead girl. Her name is Brook and she's in a rental house a couple of blocks north of the library on Lemon Lane. She's an employee of—."

"Hold up! Hold up, now!" Roy Asher jumped to his feet. "You say the girl is dead. Are you sure?" Roy looked around the lobby and there was nobody at any of the desks. He needed somebody to go get the chief.

"I'm sure. She is cold and stiff. She's in the kitchen floor and—."

"Hold on for me just a minute. Can you hold?"

"Sure. Yes."

"Chief! Chief!" Officer Asher waddled down the hallway as fast as he could and stopped in Conrad's doorway panting. "Chief, there's a guy on the phone says he found a dead girl."

Conrad looked up calmly. "Who is it?"

"That Ross guy is calling, you know, the new guy. I don't know who the girl is, but she's in a rental house on Lemon Lane."

"He's sure?"

"Yeah, he says she's stiff and cold. What do I do? Should I go out there? I can go out there and check."

Conrad sat back in his seat and looked squarely at Roy. "Get out there and radio Georgia to go to the house. Now!"

"Gotcha. Okay, Chief. Are you sure? She probably doesn't know what to do and—."

"Get out there and call Georgia!" Conrad shouted and Roy flew back down the hallway. "What did you do? Put them on hold?" Conrad yelled as he heard Roy run back to dispatch. Rolling his eyes, he pushed back from his desk and sighed. Roy could be a challenge in any role, but Conrad was glad he was not the officer responding on scene to this.

Conrad strolled down the hallway listening to Roy shriek out the details he had gathered over the radio to Georgia and then return to the telephone to tell Ross that police were on the way.

When the bluster died down and Roy's flushed face began to return to normal color, Conrad propped his hip on the corner of the desk. "So, who is the dead girl?"

"Brook. Her name is Brook and she's one of those girls up at the dress shop. She didn't show up for work today, so Ross and another girl went to check on her."

"Okay, when Georgia gets all the information together, she's going to radio you the details and ask you to contact the coroner. You know how to do that?"

"Yeah, Chief. It's right here in this book." Roy tapped a black binder in front of him where Georgia kept all of her notes and contact details.

"I'm going to head over there, but you stay here and sit tight until you hear from one of us. You got that?"

"Yep. I got it, Chief."

Conrad grabbed a few things from his office and left by the side door. He'd call Cora Mae from the car.

Saucy hopped from one foot to the other as he made his way across Fennel Street toward the Carom Seed Craft Corner with a stiff legged zigzag. That was Saucy's method of running, and although it didn't add much to his speed, it did give him a way to safely plant each foot to avoid falling and it was more than most men his age could do.

Arlene pulled the shop door open as soon as his first foot hit the sidewalk. “Saucy, come inside. What’s going on?”

Peggy saw his cheeks were pink, either from the running or from the animated conversation he’d had with Herman. “Do you want some water? Let me get you some water.”

“No, I’m fine. Thank you.” Saucy waved Peggy to stay close. “One of those girls is dead!”

“What?” Arlene grabbed her chest.

“One of those girls that works over there.” Saucy’s arm waved across the street toward Sassafras as he took several breaths before continuing. “The owner came running out and told us that she had to go. Herman Latley was supposed to do some work over there today, but she said he’d need to talk to one of the girls because she had to go.”

“Go where?” Peggy asked.

“I don’t know. Wherever the dead girl is, I guess.”

“How did she know?” Arlene looked at Peggy.

They were going to need to fill in some blanks. “She must have gotten a call.” Peggy shrugged. “They are all staying in different places around town. Someone must have found her.”

“Oh my gosh.” Arlene shuddered. “I wonder which

one. That little girl, Eden, looks fragile. She's pale as a ghost. I wonder if it was her. She just doesn't look well."

"Well, we know it wasn't Kim." Peggy looked at Saucy. "She's the one that came out and got Herman. Can I get you some water now?"

Saucy nodded. He was feeling a little light-headed and looked around until he found a chair.

Peggy returned and handed Saucy a water bottle. "Kim is the oldest. The others are all young. Maybe it was an automobile accident. Maybe she's just hurt and not really dead."

"I don't hear any sirens, do you?" Arlene looked at Peggy and then Saucy. "That's not good."

Conrad pulled his car into the driveway behind Georgia's squad car and saw Ross Miniken on the lawn with one of the other employees from Sassafras. Regina Atkins pulled up behind Conrad and blocked the driveway as soon as he got out of his car. Turning to head off Regina, he got to her car just as the door flew open.

"Good morning, Ms. Atkins. I'm going to have to ask you to leave the premises now. We will need to talk to you later, but right now we need to keep this area clear."

"She's my employee, Chief. She's my responsibility." Regina pointed to Heather and Ross on the front lawn. "They're still here!"

"They are leaving as well. We will talk to all of you later, but right now you are blocking emergency personnel's access and need to leave the premises." Conrad walked forward to block her from leaving the car.

"Chief, I need to see her! I need to know what's going on here."

"There is nothing to see. You need to go back to your store and gather her emergency contact information, so you can bring it to the police station. We will contact her family and we will update you when we can."

"But—."

"No buts. You need to leave now or you will be removed."

Regina slammed the car door and Conrad remained standing there until she started the car. When he heard the gears change, he stepped back before she ran over his feet. Driving angry was not a safe practice.

"Mr. Miniken." Conrad approached Heather and Ross with an outstretched hand. They had been introduced briefly, but he could not quite call him an acquaintance as most of his knowledge of the man was secondhand. There was much speculation being shared around town.

"Chief, this is Heather. She works at Sassafras with Brook, the young lady inside."

Conrad nodded. "We will need to take statements from each of you later, but right now we need you to return to work or home. The street must be clear for emergency personnel and there's nothing you can do here."

"We understand," Ross said as he glanced at Heather.

"I would appreciate it if you could come down to the police station this afternoon and give us a written statement, but we will be busy here for a bit longer, so maybe after lunch or mid-afternoon, if you're available."

"Sure. We can do that, Chief. We'll get out of your way now." Ross turned and tapped Heather's shoulder to lead her toward her car. Heather had not uttered a word since she saw Brook in the kitchen floor and Ross hoped some time might help her compose herself.

"Are you going back to the store?" Ross walked Heather to her car. "If you'd rather go back to your room, I'll let Regina know what's going on and I'm sure she'll understand if you need some time."

"Thank you, but I'm fine. I'm headed back to the store to let Regina know what's going on." Heather seemed to have regained her footing and although her eyes were vacant, she sounded calm and self-assured.

Ross watched as Heather pulled away from the curb and wondered where he would go. He did not want to talk to Regina right now.

"Georgia?" Conrad walked in the front door of the empty house and followed the sound of Georgia's reply.

"Hey, Chief. I called Roy and had him alert the coroner's office. I walked him through everything he needs to say, so hopefully they show up with an ambulance soon."

Conrad chuckled hearing Georgia's sigh. "Is he driving you crazy?"

"Well, I feel like I'm doing his job and mine, too. He's getting better, but it's a slow process."

"Does that surprise you?" Conrad raised an eyebrow in a mischievous smirk.

"Not at all."

"Okay then, tell me what you've got here." Conrad looked down at the young woman and around the room at the scene. There were no signs of unlawful entry, no disarray in her personal appearance, and no disorder in the kitchen.

Georgia tapped her notebook and read from her notes. "Full rigor so she's probably been dead since last night. I didn't move the body, but unless there is something underneath her, I didn't see any injury. Here's her identification." Georgia handed Conrad a

Pennsylvania driver's license that she had pulled from Brook's wallet. "No record on her."

"I sent the other two away and told them to come to the station later for statements. Her boss showed up, too, but I sent her on her way."

"The girl, Heather, seemed pretty shaken up, didn't say much. Ross Miniken was cool as a cucumber. He found her first, but Heather was right on his heels. She didn't show up for work, so they came to get her."

"How did they get inside?" Conrad walked into the empty dining room and saw the sliding door ajar.

"Ross popped the sliding door." Georgia raised both eyebrows and smiled. Not everyone knew how to do that.

Conrad's head turned when he heard car doors slam. "Sounds like someone's here."

Chapter 11

Peggy pushed through the doors of the Caraway Cafe and glanced at the table near the window, expecting to see Cora Mae and Conrad, but the table was empty. In fact, a lot of the tables were empty. Glancing at her watch, she wasn't especially early, and although the usual hustle was seen among the servers, the bustle was missing.

"Hey, Dot. Where is everybody?"

Dorothy Parish pointed to the table in the window and Peggy pulled out a chair. "You've heard about the dead girl, right?"

Peggy nodded. "Saucy told us."

"I'm guessing the word is spreading around town and I thought the cafe would be packed with people wanting window seats to the Sassafras drama, but it's just the opposite. I guess everyone is afraid to come downtown! Have you had much business this morning?"

"I didn't notice any change, but I wasn't thinking about it. Do you really think everyone knows? It's only been a few hours since they found her."

"Look around! It's not a normal day in here. It's almost noon and I'm half empty."

Peggy's forehead wrinkled in thought. "Do you think Saucy spread it all over? As far as I know, Herman Latley and Saucy were the only two that were told, other than the Sassafras girls over there. Herman's still working over there now, so unless he called or texted someone, he hasn't had much of a chance to talk about it."

"It's those scanner people! Earl Lester listens to that police radio all day long and you know Roy Asher is on dispatch this week. I've heard people in here talking about him. He's on there talking about all kinds of things he's not supposed to. I don't know anything about it really, but Jason tried to explain it to me. They have different channels and they do their private talking on one channel and then there's the public channel that Earl and his buddies follow. Apparently, Roy doesn't know the difference and he's broadcasting all kinds of crazy things. Earl is loving it." Dorothy rolled her eyes. "He had lunch here Monday and it's all he could talk about."

"Where is Jason?" Peggy looked around for

Georgia's son, Jason, who had been Frank's right hand in the kitchen for several years.

"He has moved on to greener pastures." Dorothy sighed. It was a loss she expected to happen someday, but she had been dreading it. Jason Marks had worked at the cafe since he was in high school. "He got a job at the bank and I can't fault him for taking it. They probably pay better and he does have his master's degree now. He needs to find his future, but I'm sure going to miss him."

"So, who is helping Frank?" Dorothy's husband, Frank, did all the cooking, but he had always needed help. When Jason was not working, Dorothy had filled in for him.

"I hired someone new." Dorothy's eyes widened with uncertainty. "I don't know how it's going to go, but we've got to start somewhere."

"I'm shocked you found someone. You always have trouble hiring." Peggy chuckled. "This is tough work and nobody is looking for that! Who is it?"

"Randy Little. He's not from Spicetown, but he used to work out at the Michaels' Farm on Rosemary Road. I think he grew up somewhere north of Red River."

Peggy waved at Frank when he peeked through the order window. "This may seem like easy work then, because working for Jim Michaels would have been full-on physical labor."

Dorothy held up two crossed fingers and shook them back and forth. She didn't want to work in the hot kitchen. "We'll see how it goes. He's still in the learning stages, but Frank's a good teacher. So, what did Saucy have to say? Any details?"

"No, he was just standing on the sidewalk when Regina bolted out the door. She'd just gotten a call that one of her girls was dead and she was going to the rental house. Saucy didn't even know which girl."

"Well, I do know that! It was the dark-haired girl that was in charge." Dorothy waved toward the door and Peggy turned around. "Cora's here. Maybe she can tell us."

"Maybe I can tell you what?" Cora smirked as she pulled out the chair beside Dorothy.

Dorothy jumped up from her chair. "Here, take mine. I need to get back to work, anyway. I'll get you some tea."

Cora Mae thanked her and sat down in Dorothy's chair. "I guess you were talking about the young woman from Sassafras."

"Yes! I know she was found this morning in the rental house on Lemon Lane, but I don't know why she's dead. Do you?"

"If you mean cause of death, no. I don't think anyone knows that yet, but I presume there will be an autopsy. Her family has been contacted and there was no obvious cause of death, but that's all I know."

Peggy jerked back away from the table. "No obvious cause of death? She's a young girl! They just don't keel over without cause."

"I know." Cora placed her hand over her heart and took a deep breath. "I can't imagine what could have happened to her. The Chief said she was only twenty-three."

Saucy walked by the cafe window and waved at them both. "Saucy has walked this block ten times this morning." Peggy laughed. "I guess he's waiting for Herman Latley to come out of Sassafras so he can get an update."

"What's Herman doing in there?"

"He's doing some handyman stuff for Regina. That's how Saucy knows about the body. Regina told Herman she had to go to the rental house just as he showed up for work."

"They are in there working right now?" Cora Mae pointed across the street and grimaced.

Peggy shrugged. "I guess so. I've not seen anyone leave. Regina left when she heard, but she wasn't gone long and she's back in there now. The girl that found her is back at work, too."

"Surely, they aren't really working today. Maybe they just don't have anywhere else to go. They don't really know anyone in town."

"That's true." Peggy nodded. "I've only seen two of the girls today. Kim, the older one, is in there, and Heather. Heather came back right after Regina, so I guess she is the one that found her."

"They must be traumatized."

Peggy nodded. "What's the chief going to do? Does he have any leads? Did someone break into the rental house?"

"He'll do what he does." Cora waved her hand dismissively. "Nothing for us to worry about."

Peggy hummed and glanced out the window. Maybe. Maybe not.

"Peg, your lunches are ready." Dorothy pointed at Cora Mae. "Do you want the special today?"

"Yes, please." Cora nodded to Dorothy and waved as Peggy stood up. "Tell Arlene I said hello."

"I will." Peggy nodded and jumped up to grab her order.

"Afternoon, ladies!" Saucy came through the door with a folded newspaper in his hand.

"Hi, Saucy! Would you like to join me for lunch?" Cora Mae smiled.

"I've already had my lunch, but thank you, Mayor. I just saw you in the window and wanted to ask you about something I saw in the paper today."

Cora Mae's brow furrowed quizzically. "What's in

there?" She had glanced through the paper and didn't remember anything significant.

"Maybe you know about it, but it looks like that railroad guy you have coming in September is buying people's train sets. There's a number in here you can call for an appraisal from them." Saucy handed Cora the folded paper and pointed at the classified ad.

"Hmm, I didn't know anything about this, but it is the same name. The person I've talked to is Mr. Abbott. I can check at the office and see if the number is the same."

"Well, if it is the same guy, I'm going to give him a call, and see what he thinks about my trains. They might be worth something!"

"Oh, I've been meaning to tell you, Saucy." Cora Mae winced. "I'm really sorry, but the railroad show isn't going to be coming in September. I never could work it out with Mr. Abbott. He needed things that I just couldn't arrange for him, and we decided that we were not a good fit for his show."

"Aw, shucks! I was looking forward to that!"

Saucy looked out the window with a forlorn expression that broke Cora Mae's heart. "I know you were and I hate it, but I'll keep my eyes open for another opportunity."

"Okay, I understand." Saucy's head lowered. "I still may try to give this guy a call."

"But I'll check after lunch for you and send you a text about the phone number. I wouldn't want you to call someone and it turn out to be a con artist."

"Okie doke! Thanks, Mayor."

Chapter 12

"I want you to have the first round with Regina." Conrad handed a notebook to Georgia. "I've got a few questions set up for you to start with. I think a fresh face will help ease her anxiety. We have a bit of a history." Conrad chuckled.

"Okay, Chief." Georgia scanned the questions on the pad.

"I'm going to talk to Heather." Conrad smiled. "I haven't had any arguments with her before."

"Ah, Chief! You never let me question anybody!" Roy's lower lip was out and his nose crinkled in disappointment. Georgia grabbed a blank pad of paper and a pen, trying to get out of the middle of the conversation.

"Holler if you need me," Conrad said to Georgia as

she reached for the doorknob of Interview Room 1.

Strolling over to the dispatch cubicle, Conrad patted Briscoe on the head when he opened one eye to check Conrad's movement. "I have to make a judgment call on the best interview technique, and Georgia is the best person for this interview. Every situation is different, Roy. You'll get your chance." Conrad hoped that only happened after he retired. "It's not personal."

Roy scowled, but turned back towards the desk when the phone rang, and Conrad stepped quickly to Interview Room 2, where Heather waited for him.

"Afternoon," Conrad said as he pulled out a chair to sit across the table from Heather. "I don't think we've formally met, but I'm Chief Harris."

"Hi, yes. I'm Heather Halstrom." Heather bobbed her head nervously as her eyes darted around the room. Her plump cheeks were as shiny as an apple that had been rubbed on his sleeve, and her eyes were dry. No puffiness or weariness to be seen.

"I understand you found your colleague, Brook, this morning at her rental house."

Heather nodded.

"Can you tell me about your day beginning when you showed up at work, please?" Conrad pushed his chair back a little to put his notebook in his lap. "I'm going to take a few notes here. Just start with arriving at the store. What time was it?"

“I got there a few minutes before eight. Regina was the only one there at first, but the other girls started showing up right after that.”

“You’re an early morning person!” Conrad glanced up and smiled.

“Not really.” Heather smirked. “I just believe in being on time.”

“Ah, I see. Okay, everyone trickled in except Brook. When did you notice that?”

Heather frowned. “I guess I really didn’t. Regina said something about it and she sent Kim upstairs to see if Brook was there. She said Brook was supposed to be making some calls for her to other stores, so she might be upstairs. Until then, I hadn’t missed her.”

“Did Brook have different job duties than the rest of the group?”

“Not really. We all just do whatever Regina tells us to.”

“Oh, I thought Brook was different. I thought she was in charge of things.” Conrad narrowed his eyes when he caught a slight stiffening in Heather’s posture.

“Oh, Regina calls her the lead worker, but that doesn’t really mean anything on this trip. See, usually the lead worker stays behind and runs the store, so they’re more involved in the setup because it’s going to be their own place, but that’s not the case this time. Regina is staying behind, so the lead worker title doesn’t mean anything."

"She didn't direct your work or tell you what to do?"

Heather's eyebrows shot up and she shook her head. "No, she didn't."

"Okay, what happened after Regina realized she wasn't there?"

Heather sighed. "Well, she tried to call her I think or text her. I wasn't really paying attention, but then at one point she said someone needed to go to her rental and wake her up. I guess she thought she slept in. Regina couldn't leave because she was waiting on a handyman, so I volunteered."

"Why was that?"

"Why was what?" Heather's nose wrinkled.

"Why did you volunteer?"

"Oh! Well, I knew where the rental was and I wasn't busy with anything else yet. I don't know. I just volunteered." Heather shrugged and seemed puzzled herself.

"Was Ross Miniken there when all this happened?"

"No, he came later. You see, I went to the house and banged on all the doors, but she wouldn't answer, so I called Regina and told her."

"Was Ross there then?"

"I don't know, but Regina said she was going to call the real estate guy that rented the place to us. He would have a key. I waited and then she texted me to say Ross was coming instead."

Conrad tilted his chin up in thought. "Do you know Ross Miniken? Did that seem odd to you? Did you think Ross had a key?"

"I don't know. I guess I just thought he was coming to help. He stops by the store every day, so I kinda' know him." Heather shrugged and lifted one corner of her mouth.

Conrad had been puzzled by Ross Miniken's involvement from the start. "Ross and Regina are friends?"

"Yeah, I guess." Heather added another shrug with obvious indifference.

"So, Ross shows up." Conrad nodded and looked to the side. "And the two of you break into the house?"

Heather sat up straight. "No. It wasn't like that. He tried knocking and stuff, just like I had, but nothing worked. Then he mentioned trying the back door. I told him I'd already been around there but the curtain was pulled shut to the sliding glass door. I couldn't see in. We went around and looked at it and then he went to his car and got a screwdriver."

"What did you think he was going to do?"

"Well, I didn't think anything, really." Heather's blank stare confirmed that.

"So, he came back with the screwdriver and popped the sliding glass door?"

"Yeah!"

"Were you there watching?" Conrad tilted his head in confusion, but not at Ross's actions. He was confused by her guilty reaction.

"I was, but I have never seen anybody do that before. It's kinda' scary that it's that easy to do."

Conrad nodded. It was a very common entry spot for burglars and he thought most people were unaware of how easy it was to bypass the lock. He couldn't help but wonder how Ross was so familiar with it though.

"So, the door is open now. Tell me what happened next."

"Nothing much. Ross went in and I followed him. He went left to the kitchen and I went right to the living room, but she wasn't in there, so I came in the kitchen and Ross had already found her."

"Did you touch her?"

Heather recoiled. "Absolutely not!"

"Why didn't you call 9-1-1?"

"Because Ross said she was dead."

Conrad scratched his chin. "So, Ross touched her?"

"I guess so. I didn't watch." Heather's head shook with a shudder. "I think he was already calling the police by then."

"Okay, did you look around the rest of the house while you were waiting?" Conrad lifted his eyebrows.

Heather's eyes were vacant again. "I don't think so.

No, I just went back outside and waited. I don't remember anything else."

"Did you call Regina?"

"No, Ross did that, too, I think. He took care of everything. I'm so glad he was there. I wouldn't have known what to do."

"Tell me about Brook. How long have you known her?" Conrad sat back in his chair. He'd always had the sense that none of the girls really liked each other, or Regina for that matter. They didn't cluster and whisper together when he and Regina would trade words. They would gawk, but they didn't comment. They all seemed to exist independently of each other.

"I worked one other job with her earlier in the year, but I don't really know her. She's fairly new, but Regina likes her."

"So, you've worked for Regina longer than Brook?" Conrad made a note on his pad.

"Oh, yeah. I've done these jobs for Regina lots of times! I've helped her set up five or six stores over the last couple of years." Heather's mood lifted and she smiled.

"What do you do between these setup jobs?"

"I work in one of her stores in Middlebrook. I've worked there for almost five years. These trips pay really well and not everybody can do them because they can't be gone from home for several weeks."

Conrad nodded. “So, Brook worked in one of her other stores, too?”

Heather’s eyebrows came together and she paused. “I don’t really know where she came from. She talked like she worked for Regina all the time though, but I never asked her.”

“It doesn’t sound like you guys are very close. Do you know her last name?” Conrad grinned impishly.

“Um,” Heather said as her eyes looked around the room. “Calvert! That’s it. Brook Calvert.” Heather’s soft chuckle confirmed she was proud of herself.

“Well done!” Conrad laughed. “I don’t suppose you know whether she had any thoughts or any reason to consider suicide, do you?”

Heather’s mouth fell open. “You think she killed herself?”

“Oh, I don’t know.” Conrad shrugged. “I’m just asking.”

“I don’t know her that well. I mean, she seemed happy enough, I guess. We never talked about stuff. She’s not a friend. I just work with her.”

“So, you’ve been around her a couple of weeks now, and you worked with her a month or two earlier in the year, but you don’t really know her.” Conrad restated the sentiment she was sharing, but he found it hard to believe she knew so little. “Even if you didn’t talk, I’m sure you formed opinions about her. What kind of person did she seem like to you?"

Heather chewed her bottom lip and looked to her left. "She was nice enough. Sometimes she could be a little bossy, but she was just trying to impress Regina." Heather pushed out her lower lip and seemed unable to come up with any other ideas. "She was okay, I guess."

"Did everyone in the group get along well?" Conrad heard the door shut to the room next door.

"For the most part. Eden didn't like Brook at all, but everybody else seemed okay with her. I don't know."

"You've said 'I don't know' and 'I guess' about a dozen times so far. Can you tell me something you feel certain you know about Brook Calvert?" Conrad leaned forward with his elbows on the table.

Heather looked down at her hands as she bounced both of her legs under the table. When she looked back up, Conrad saw a light suddenly in her eyes. "She wanted to move up. She wanted to be promoted or get her own store, or whatever Regina had to offer. She wanted advancement."

Conrad nodded in satisfaction. "I'm going to grab some water. Can I get you something?"

Heather shook her head. "No, thank you."

"I'll be right back." Conrad slipped out of the interview room door and motioned for Georgia to follow him to his office.

Chapter 13

"Have a seat." Conrad pointed as he reached for his coffee cup to top it off with some fresh chicory from his coffee maker. "What did you find out?"

"Well, Chief, she doesn't have a great memory for what happened yesterday. They had a luncheon at the store and everyone was working on different jobs at different places around the building, so her story isn't very fluid. Brook spent a few hours in the afternoon with her while they went over inventory reports from the other stores. She was going to have Brook make some calls to those stores this morning to get certain items shipped to them here. The rest of the gang was busy putting up displays and opening boxes to unpack supplies and merchandise."

"So, they had lunch together?"

"Not really. It sounds like they all just snacked all day. Some sat down to eat while others worked and everyone just did their own thing. They aren't a cohesive group, but everybody did contribute something as far as she could remember."

"Did you get through all the questions?" Conrad had roughed out a few ideas of what he would have asked, but things always took a life of their own once you started questioning someone.

"I did. She said Brook has worked for her this year, but used to work for her brother, Garrett, as a receptionist in his office. Her brother is a financial partner in Sassafras, but he doesn't get involved in overseeing the stores. Regina does all that."

"But she kept her on all year, so she must have been doing a good job." Conrad hoped that meant Regina knew her better than Heather did.

"Yes, she said she was doing an excellent job. She said she was smart and energetic, always willing to pitch in wherever she was needed."

"Hmm, some of that could be just the death glow. Everyone seems more wonderful after they're gone. It's hard to tell when they are just trying not to say anything bad, or if it was genuinely that rosy."

Georgia tipped her head to the side and squinted her eyes. "It might have had a little whipped cream on top, but I got the feeling she did a good job, enough that the other girls were jealous. Regina said none of the other girls were friendly to her and sometimes refused to do what she told them to do. They saw Brook as the boss's pet and resented her for it."

"Did Regina know anything about her personal life?"

"No, Regina barely knows those girls' names!" Georgia huffed. "She said no suicidal ideation or allergies, to her knowledge, which doesn't mean much."

"And the Ross Miniken connection?" Conrad stood up from the desk chair and took another drink.

"They're friends. She says she just met him here in Spicetown and he's a nice guy. She mentioned he was planning to stop by the station after he got back in town this afternoon. He had an appointment in Paxton."

"Huh," Conrad said as he abandoned his coffee again. "I'll go see what Heather remembers about last night."

"Do you see anything?" Peggy walked over to the front store window, looking up and down Fennel Street, and pointed across the street. "Anybody coming or going?"

"Not since Regina left." Arlene shook her head and joined Peggy at the window. "I never saw Heather come back either."

"I wonder what's going on over there." Peggy's forehead wrinkled in thought. "I had hoped maybe one of them would run over here to grab their leftovers. It's after lunchtime and I'm sure they're getting hungry."

"They must be traumatized." Arlene shook her head. "Regina comes in and tells them their friend is dead before running back out. I'm sure they have a million questions."

"She must be down at the police station. Heather must be there, too, I guess."

"I think the only thing in our refrigerator right now is their meat tray. The round platter with cold cuts and cheese is on the bottom shelf. They didn't bring the pies back." Arlene looked at the clock on the wall.

"Maybe I should run this meat platter across the street to them. Somebody needs to check on them, and I might be able to find out what's happened so far." Peggy walked toward the storage room.

"You can take a few of my cold drinks from in there, too." Arlene's voice trailed off as she saw a large panel van pull up in front of Sassafras and she yelled out to Peggy. "There's a van over there now."

Returning with the meat tray and a plastic bag of drinks, Peggy glanced out the window. "Duncan's

Appliance Village. That must be the refrigerators Regina ordered. She was looking for cheap used models to put in the storage room of the store and one for her apartment upstairs."

"How long do you think this truck will block the street?" Arlene rolled her eyes.

"I'll run over there and snoop a little. Text me if you need me."

Arlene held the door open for Peggy and stood in the doorway as she paused for a passing car while the car behind the appliance van waited to go around.

"Oh, excuse me!" The driver popped around the side of the truck and startled Peggy.

"I'm sorry. I didn't see you there. You know, there is an alley in the back. It might be easier for you to deliver back there." Peggy smiled and shrugged her shoulders innocently. "That way the drivers won't get so testy with you."

"Really? Ah, thanks. I may do that. Does it go all the way through?"

Peggy nodded and looked up as Kim walked out to the truck.

"Hey, Peggy. You brought our lunch? That was so nice of you! Thank you."

"Oh, you're welcome. I saw you had things going on over here so I thought I'd run it over on my way to pick up our lunch. I'll just take it inside and get out of your way." Peggy darted in the door, hearing snatches of conversation about refrigerators and alleys behind her, concerned she had picked a bad time to visit.

"Hello, ladies!" Peggy walked toward the counter and slid the meat tray down the center of the cash wrap. "I brought your lunch meat over. I thought you might be getting hungry."

"Wow! Thank you." Missy removed the plastic cover and placed it on a nearby desk. "Can you bring the bread out, Eden?"

Eden walked out of the back room with bread, chips, and napkins. "It's not fancy, but I'm hungry."

"I'm so glad to see the refrigerator is here. We can't even keep drinks cold. I'm running over to the bakery three or four times a day for refills." Missy grabbed a napkin and opened the loaf of bread.

"Vicki will surely miss your business!" Peggy smiled. "I didn't know how much food you had left over for today, but hopefully it is enough to make a decent lunch. I know you've had a traumatic morning and I have to commend you for trying to work through it."

Missy's face flashed a brief expression of distress as she nodded.

"You mean about Brook?" Eden reached in the chip bag and pulled out a handful of potato chips, launching one into her mouth before turning the bag toward Missy.

"Yes, I heard that she died this morning, and I was

shocked. Has she been ill?"

Eden shrugged. "Not that I know about. We haven't been told anything other than she was found dead. Regina and Heather are down there talking to the cops about it."

"Regina just ran in and out quickly. I think we were too stunned to ask questions and she didn't offer any details. She wanted to make sure we knew what needed to get done this morning, so we've been trying to get things set up for her. I don't know when she'll be back."

"Eden, can you move that box?" Kim yelled out as she held the front door open. "The fridge is coming through this way."

Peggy pushed a few smaller boxes away from the center of the room with her foot to clear an area for the handcart to pass through. Apparently the delivery person didn't take her advice to use the alley. "Are they delivering two refrigerators?"

"Yeah," Kim said as she pointed up the stairway. "The other one goes upstairs."

"Come on. I'll show you where it goes." Eden turned to lead the delivery boy to the back room with a sandwich in one hand and chips in another.

"Are there a lot of murders around here?" Missy looked at Peggy. "I mean, should we be worried about being out after dark?"

"Murders? Was Brook murdered?" Peggy's eyes

widened.

Missy hesitated and looked at Kim guiltily. “I don’t know. I just assumed—.”

“We don’t know that. We don’t know anything.” Kim’s eyebrows knitted together in a scolding glance. “We just know Brook was found dead this morning. That’s all. It could have been an accident or maybe she was sick and we just didn’t know it.”

Peggy nodded. “I’m sure there is an explanation and Regina will fill you in when she returns. Spicetown does not have a lot of murders. I can assure you of that.”

“What do you consider a lot?” Missy’s eyes squinted in question.

Peggy blinked slowly. “Well...” Peggy was looking back in her memories. The dead guy at the Nutmeg Inn didn’t really count because he overdosed accidentally and the dead guy at the community center construction site wasn’t really intentionally killed. “It’s probably been a couple of years since we’ve had a real murder in town.”

Missy tilted her head. “How do you define a *real* murder?”

“Enough! No more talk of murder.” The appliance delivery guy jumped at Kim’s outburst and then pushed the empty handcart toward the door. “Missy, please go hold the door open for him. The next one has to go up the stairs.”

“I need to get back to the store,” Peggy said as she

pulled her phone from her back pocket. “Come on over later if there’s anything we can do for you. Take care, girls, and don’t work too hard.”

Chapter 14

"Heather, I'm going to let you go for now, but I need you to spend some time reflecting on the details of what has happened in the last twenty-four hours. I've asked you a lot of questions and you have told me dozens of times that you don't remember or you don't know. I need something more tangible than that. Your accounting of Brook's last few hours is very important. Do you understand that?"

Heather dropped her head and frowned. "Yeah. I just need some time. Too much has happened. I can't think."

"I'll ask Regina if you can have the afternoon off to go back to your room and make some notes if that will help, or you can stay here. I can give you some privacy in this room and you can try to write down the events. I don't want too much time to pass or you will forget the details."

"What about the other girls? They were there. Are you going to talk to them, too?"

"I plan to talk to everyone. Is there someone in particular who might be helpful?" Conrad leaned forward with his elbows on his knees. Heather's responses had deteriorated the more he asked of her and she'd become whiny and uncooperative. He needed her to pull things together and offer something that made some sense.

"Kim. Kim knows everything and she's always in the middle of whatever we're doing. She'll remember who was doing what yesterday."

"Okay. Anyone else?"

"Eden hates Brook, so she stays away from her and I don't think Missy pays attention to what's going on around her much, so they may not be much help. Regina was there most of the time though."

"Most of the time? Did she leave for part of the day?" Conrad leaned back in his chair.

"She went upstairs sometimes and made calls. I don't know if she was there all day or not. We don't all stay in one place. Some of us work upstairs, some downstairs, and some are in the storeroom in the back. There's a lot of different stuff to do."

"You said Brook was there all day, but what about the evening? Did you talk or see each other after work?"

"We are all staying in different places, so we just leave separately."

"What about dinner? Do you have your evening meal together when you're done working?"

Heather shook her head. "Not last night. We did the night before because Ross invited us all out together, but usually we just go our own way."

Conrad stood up. "So, the last time you saw Brook alive was yesterday at the end of your work shift. Is that correct?"

"Yes," Heather said, confidently. "And she was fine."

Conrad asked Heather to give him a few minutes and he stepped out into the hallway where Georgia was waiting. "Hey, Georgia. Are you done with her?"

"Yeah, Chief. She's getting testy and she doesn't have much to say. She keeps telling me how much she has to do and that she needs to get back to the store." Georgia handed Conrad her notes and he glanced at the lack of answers. No one seemed to have much to add.

"Tabor is fingerprinting the house and bagging the evidence. There are three girls still at the store to talk to, but I'll run down there this afternoon. You can grab some lunch now and I'll let these two go after I have a word with Regina."

"Okay, Chief." Georgia turned toward Roy Asher, who was sitting in the dispatch cubicle listening to them.

"Roy, you'll need to call over to the coroner's office in about an hour and ask who caught this case. The chief will need to know who is assigned to her."

"Okay," Roy said as he wrote himself a note.

"Oh, and if they say there's no assignment yet, tell them the chief would like Alice Warner if she's available."

Roy looked at Conrad for confirmation. "Gotcha."

"Then let the chief know who it is." Georgia spun on her heel to walk toward the side door after Roy nodded.

Conrad glanced between Roy and Georgia and huffed. "I've always wondered how that worked." Conrad reached for the interview room doorknob and watched Roy smile before spinning his chair around to grab the ringing phone. He might just get the hang of all this dispatch stuff, eventually.

Regina twitched in surprised when Conrad walked into the room. "Chief! I hope you are telling me I can get back to work now. I really need to get back to the store."

"I understand that and that's why I had Officer Marks talk with you to save time, but I do have a couple of questions for you."

"Sure. What can I do for you?"

Conrad smiled at her sarcasm and kept his hand on the doorknob. "What do you think killed Brook Calvert?"

Regina straightened up in her chair. "How do I know? Isn't that your job? I have no idea!"

"No idea at all? A young twenty-three-year-old girl dies suddenly. You've spent forty hours a week around this girl for the last two years and you have no guesses?"

"No! I mean maybe she slipped and hit her head. Maybe she had a heart condition we didn't know about or had an aneurysm. I have no idea."

"Hmm," Conrad nodded with conviction. "Second question. Who do you think would like to see Brook Calvert dead?"

"Nobody! This is ridiculous, Chief. Nobody would kill Brook! Why would you even ask such a question? I'm sure this was all an accident or a...."

"A what?" Conrad raised an eyebrow.

"I don't know, but this isn't a murder investigation. It is a horrible thing that's happened to a beautiful, young girl, but nobody murdered Brook. It has to be a terrible accident."

"Why do you think that? Do you think beautiful, young people don't get murdered? Because they do, every day." Conrad was toying with her now. Regina Adkins had to be in control of everything and expected everyone to follow her lead. Her arrogance brought out the worst in Conrad and they had gotten off on the wrong foot when she'd arrived in town.

"I know that, Chief." Regina sighed and centered her emotions to accept defeat. "I just feel like this is a freak situation, an accident or an illness no one knew about. Brook didn't have any enemies. No one would benefit from her death. She had nothing that anyone else wanted and she was kind to everyone."

Conrad sensed he was at a dead end and antagonizing Regina further would not benefit the case. "I'm going to stop by this afternoon and talk to the other girls if there is time after Mr. Miniken's statement. If not, I'll be there tomorrow morning, but you can go now."

Regina stood up and grabbed her purse. "Thank you." Pushing past Conrad, she left quickly and he glanced at the clock. He had missed lunch with Cora at the cafe, but he had one more question for Heather.

When Conrad walked back into Heather's interview room, she was scrolling through her phone and absorbed in whatever she was reading. "Ms. Halstrom." Conrad pulled out a chair. "I apologize for the delay."

"Oh, no problem," Heather said without looking up and then put her phone back in her purse. "Can I go now?"

"Did you think about that statement? Do you want the afternoon off or would you like to have some time here to think?"

"Nah. I need to get back to the store." Heather pushed her chair back as she stood up. "With Brook gone, Regina is going to be shorthanded. She's going to need me there."

"Wait. Before you go, there is one more thing I forgot to ask you."

"Yeah?" Heather put her hand on the back of her chair and stared at Conrad.

Conrad stood and pushed his chair under the table. "What food did you bring to the luncheon yesterday?"

Heather looked down at the table and pushed her chair in before answering. "Chips and dip."

"And Brook? Do you remember what she brought?"

Heather frowned and put her purse strap over her shoulder. "I'm not sure. It might have been a dessert. We had a lot of them though, so I can't say for sure."

Conrad's eyes narrowed at her answer. He saw something in her hesitation that made him think she was intentionally being vague. Regina had answered the same question according to Georgia's notes and he wondered why Heather struggled with it. "Okay, we'll talk again tomorrow. I'm hoping you will have remembered a bit more by then."

"I'll try." Heather walked around the table and reached for the doorknob.

Conrad held the door open as she walked out. "I'll see you again soon."

Heather did not look back as she walked through the lobby and out the front door. Conrad walked to the dispatch cubicle and looked down at Briscoe who was sound asleep in his dog bed under the counter. “Roy, I’m going to the cafe for lunch. If Ross Miniken comes in, tell him I’m at lunch and ask him to wait here for me.”

“Sure thing, Chief.”

“Tabor and Georgia should be back soon. Text me if you need anything.”

Chapter 15

Peggy ambled across Fennel Street in a blur of confusion and disappointment. The girls seemed calm and had been productively working all morning. She hadn't seen a single indication of concern for Brook from any of them and she had at least expected some fake theatrics. There was evidence of their progress in the boxes and packaging strewn around the room, but no evidence of sadness. Except for Missy's fixation on her own safety, they had all seemed focused only on getting the job done. How dismal it must be to work all week among people that couldn't be bothered to care whether you lived or died.

Arlene rushed back to the window as Peggy walked through the door. "Perfect timing. Regina just walked by the appliance delivery truck after you left. I guess she had to park over in the next block. Still no sign of Heather. Did you find out anything?"

Peggy took a deep breath before propping her elbow on the counter. "Well, I found out that those girls were hungry, so they were happy for the food, but otherwise everything is business as usual over there."

"What? Do they know what happened?" Arlene's outrage straightened her back and flared her nostrils. "What were they doing over there when you walked in?"

"Oh, they know, but Regina didn't tell them anything more than what we know. They are over there working away on their assigned chores and don't seem to have any concerns about Brook."

"That sounds a little heartless." Arlene huffed. "I would have expected a bigger reaction than that."

"Well, Missy is worried about herself. She asked if Spicetown had a lot of murders, but none of them really mentioned Brook at all."

"Pfft, what a silly thought. Spicetown is the safest place in the world." Arlene grabbed an oatmeal raisin cookie from the bakery box on the counter and pushed herself up onto the bar stool behind the cash register.

"I guess I was just startled that there were no tears or panic at all."

"I know young people have their own unique ideas about the world, but I would hate to think they are so desensitized to death that it's become meaningless to them."

"It was almost as if it was old news." Peggy pictured herself walking over there two weeks after Brook's death and bringing it up to the store clerk. No, even then she would have expected them to act more affected than these girls did today. "They aren't a close group."

"Maybe they didn't like her!" Arlene held a napkin under her chin preparing to take a bite when her arm shot out in front of her to point out the front window with her cookie. "There goes Heather."

"I hope this truck moves soon. I wanted to give Sully a short walk and I'm not walking down the alley again." Peggy reached in the box for a cookie. "Did you get any replies to your email about the knitting group?"

"I did! I've gotten a reply from Dorleen, Mildred, and Joyce. They plan to be here. Leona wasn't sure yet and Julia hasn't answered. I was hoping Grace and Cora might come too."

"We'll need to rearrange a few things to get some extra chairs in the back. I was hoping to show them some samples of cross stitch patterns from that software I have, but it's not going as well as I'd hoped."

Arlene brushed the crumbs from her fingers. "Why? Are the printouts hard to read?"

"They are, but the photos are just too complex. It prints out ten pages long with twenty color choices, and I think our town is just too colorful for this experiment."

Arlene laughed. "Does every box need a different thread color?"

"It does! It would drive me mad. I've got to find something more simplistic to use as an example."

"Have you tried using a photo of one of Sonjay's paintings yet? They might have less color change than a real-life photo."

"I haven't tried that yet." Peggy rubbed her hands together over the wastebasket to remove the crumbs from her fingers. "I thought about maybe just our sign. I could make a pattern of just our store sign and we could stitch that and hang it behind the register. What do you think?"

"That's a great idea! Make one for the Salty Shipper too, and I'll stitch one for the other side."

Peggy nodded and pulled out her phone to add herself a reminder to place an order with Vicki at the bakery for more cookies for next week's knitting group.

Conrad tossed his lunch on his desk. A foot-long sub sandwich from Sesame Subs was not ideal, but it was fast. He had hoped for some time to think a bit on the morning's events, but Ross Miniken had shown up shortly after he left for lunch and Roy had sent him a text message.

"Hey, Roy. I'm back." Conrad saw Eugene Tabor had also returned and was sitting at his desk. The desk next to him was covered with evidence bags all sealed and labeled.

"Oh, hey Chief. He's in Room 2." Asher pointed to the interview room. "I told him you'd be right back."

"Thank you, Roy. Did you get everything, Tabor?"

"Yeah, Chief. It's all here. I'm putting together an inventory list now."

"Thanks." Conrad reached for the doorknob to Room 2, still debating where to begin. Ross Miniken's involvement in this didn't make sense.

"Good afternoon, Mr. Miniken. I appreciate you finding the time to stop by."

"Of course, Chief. I know what you want to ask about and I don't blame you. You don't have to tell me. I know I should have handled it differently. I don't know what I was thinking. I never thought things would go the way they did, and I was just trying to help out the girls. I know I should have called the station when Brook wouldn't answer the door."

"Let's back up a little." Conrad pulled out a chair and sat across the table from Ross. "How did you meet

Regina and her staff?"

Ross smiled smugly and leaned back in his chair. "We met at the Nutmeg Inn. We're both staying there and once we started talking, we realized we have a lot in common. We're both new in town and trying to establish a new business and a home."

Conrad nodded.

Ross leaned forward with his elbows on the table and tilted his head. "No offense, but we've both had a few problems fitting in around here. The locals aren't all as welcoming as we expected. Having each other has helped us get through it."

"I was not aware you were having difficulties." Conrad raised an eyebrow in inquiry. He would like to hear this story. He'd never known anyone to find Spicetown unfriendly but if it was true, there must be a reason.

"I had a difficult time renting that storefront and I've still not found a house. I think Regina has had it harder than I have. She's asked a number of the store owners nearby for help and they have been reluctant. I think she's feeling alienated. It helped us to have a friendly ear. I've tried to help a little around her store and she has offered to help me decorate my office a little once she gets set up."

"I see, so that's why she called you instead of the police this morning?" Conrad made a few notes on the notepad he had on his knee. He would have to ask the store owners if there was any reason for their lack of support.

"No. No, I just popped in at the right time!"

"Popped in?"

"The store. I popped in to say good morning and found her in a panic. She'd just gotten a call from Heather that she was at Brook's rental, but she couldn't get Brook to come to the door. I volunteered to go see if I could help."

"No mention of calling the police? No concern that something was wrong?"

"Oh, she was concerned, but no one ever thought she might be dead. Who thinks a young healthy girl will turn up dead?"

"Who indeed?" Conrad smirked.

"And Regina was a little hesitant to call the station. I know she's had some run-ins with you and she probably wasn't sure you wanted to help her." Ross threw his hands up with his palms out. "That's just my assumption. She didn't say that."

Conrad dismissed the issue with a sniff and tapped his pen on his paper. "Let's get to the part where you arrive at the house. Where was Heather?"

"Waiting for me by her car. She explained to me that she'd tried the bell and knocked without success, but I tried it again myself. When it didn't work, I mentioned the back of the house and she told me she'd been there, too. We walked around back and the curtain was pulled on the back door, but I thought we could probably get in."

"You have experience breaking into sliding doors?"

"A little." Ross chuckled, although his body seemed to tense. "I locked myself out of my own house once and watched a tutorial on YouTube to learn how to do it. I'm not a pro at it, but since there wasn't a bar in the track, I thought we had a chance."

"Go on." Conrad made a note on his pad of Ross' admission, but he had a strong suspicion that it wasn't truthful.

"I got a screwdriver from my car and it got us in. I found her in the kitchen floor and then I called the police station."

"If the message I got was correct, you told the dispatch officer that the body was stiff and cold." It was just a statement, but Conrad hoped Ross would pick up on the implied question.

"Hmm, I can't really remember what I said." Ross' eyes roamed the ceiling of the room. "The heat of the moment, you know." The simple shrug was stiff and Ross' face was flushed with nerves.

"You touched her?" Conrad spelled it out. "What exactly did you do when you found her?"

Ross' chest heaved from an extended sigh. "I think

I ran over and reached for her neck, but I knew instantly. I didn't really search for a pulse then. She was cold to the touch and her head did not move."

"Was Heather there when you did this?"

"I think she was behind me. I yelled at her as soon as I saw Brook in the floor but then my back was turned. I think Heather came into the room while I was down there."

Conrad leaned forward with a penetrating glare and waited for Ross to meet his gaze. Ross had lost eye contact with him through that description and he seemed to be swimming in uncertainty. "Were you kneeling, bending over, or squatted down?"

Ross' forehead crinkled in alarm. "I'm not sure. Maybe all three. It happened so fast. Is that important?"

Conrad ignored the question. "Did your body make contact with Brook's? Maybe your knee was at her hip or your leg touched her side."

Ross shook his head and his shoulders slumped in disappointment.

"You violated a crime scene when you approached her and we need to know what possible contact you made. The tips of your fingers, the sole of your shoes, any of your movements might disturb evidence at the scene and cause an unwanted transfer of material."

Ross rubbed his fingertips across his eyelids to his temples. "Oh my gosh! I'm so sorry, Chief. I didn't even think about that. It was just a reaction and I never meant to harm anything. I didn't expect what I found and I thought she was just injured."

"I hope you can see why it would have been best for everyone if you or Regina had called us."

"I do, of course, and if I could go back in time..."

"Not to mention breaking in someone else's home is never a good look." Conrad looked down at his pad, but knew his sneer was uncontrolled. He'd had enough fun with the new guy. "Now, tell me what you know about the girls working for Regina."

Chapter 16

Cora Mae Bingham walked into the Juniper Junction restaurant and looked around the room while she waited for the hostess. Conrad was parking the car and it had been months since they had gone out for a quiet dinner. Her work had been busy with holidays and events throughout the summer, and now he had a death case to solve. She was anxious to hear all about it.

The hostess walked up just as Conrad walked through the front door and she led them to a quiet booth against the far wall.

"Did you have difficulty finding a parking place?" Cora opened her menu and lowered it to the table.

"No, I'm just a little down the street near Peggy's shop. There's a street lamp out across the street down there where I parked though, so you probably need to let

Rodney know."

Cora pulled her phone from her purse to tap in a reminder for Monday. "I think I spied Saucy sitting in the back of the room when we walked through. I can't tell who he's with, but he never misses a chance to come here. We should probably do this more often. The atmosphere is relaxing."

"Be better if they had steak." Conrad put his reading glasses on and studied the menu. His stomach couldn't tolerate too much spice and he didn't want to be up all night.

"Variety is good!" Cora closed her menu and put it on the edge of the table. "Speaking of variety, what's going on with the Sassafras death?"

"Alice called me right before I left the office. She hasn't had time to do much, but her initial impression is that it was a reaction to a toxin. She's running all the tests now, but they take time."

"Something from the store, maybe?" Cora squinted her eyes. "They are opening a lot of boxes coming from various distributors and other stores. It could be anything."

Conrad nodded. "Her parents said she didn't have any health problems and no one else is sick, but it's possible she had a sensitivity to some chemical and just didn't know it. Alice said she'd test for everything."

Their conversation paused while the server took

their order. Conrad stayed safe with the butter chicken, and Cora Mae decided to be adventurous with a new dish. When the server walked away, Cora saw that Saucy had almost made his way to the front door.

“Is Saucy with Mr. Abbott?” Cora pointed at the exit. “He said he might call him for an appraisal.”

“I thought that guy was long gone.” Conrad leaned out of the booth and saw them walk down the sidewalk by the front windows. “Yep, that’s Abbott.”

“I’ll have to ask Saucy about that when I see him next.” The server brought their drinks and Cora thanked him. “Okay, now tell me what you think about the Sassafras ladies. I just met them today and it was just a brief introduction.”

“Have you been in the store?”

“Yes, I stopped in late in the day to share my condolences. I met Regina briefly several weeks ago, but I didn’t know her employees.”

“Well,” Conrad groaned as he leaned back against the booth. “They don’t work as a team. Frankly, I don’t think they even know each other very well. Regina pulls them all together from different places and sends them to set up a new store. A few had worked together briefly on another project, but they aren’t close.”

“I would think it would be difficult to just pick up and go somewhere to work with strangers for a few weeks. I wonder what the incentive is to volunteer. Does

Regina pay them extra?"

"It pays extra." Conrad nodded and then frowned. "It may also be for advancement. One of the girls said that the store manager was usually selected from the set-up team."

"Oh! So, the set-up is a trial for them?" Cora shrugged. "It makes sense, I guess."

"One of them told me that whoever is lead for the set-up usually gets the manager's job, but this trip is different because Regina told them after they got here that she thought she would just stay and manage this store."

"Were they all disappointed?" Cora Mae stirred her tea and looked over as the waiter carried a tray past their table.

"She wasn't. She doesn't want to move, but the others might have been. Kim seems to have the opinion that the trip is a time to shine and be considered for future advancement. She's new on this trip. It's her first one."

"None of the ladies seemed upset by Brook's death." It had been awkward when Cora shared her sympathy with them and her words were met with blank stares.

"Eden hated Brook, so she can't muster a tear. Kim and Missy seemed saddened, maybe mildly alarmed, but you're right. They weren't invested in any friendship with Brook. She was Regina's favorite in their eyes, so there might have been a little jealousy there."

Cora Mae leaned back in her seat when their order arrived and spread her napkin in her lap. She cut into her Tandoori Chicken and watched the steam rise. "What about the young girl that found her?"

"Heather." Conrad stabbed at his chicken. "She had nothing to offer and she wasn't particularly traumatized by the situation. Most people are shaken by finding a dead body even if it is someone they've never met. I still remember the first one I saw."

"I know I certainly was, but I'm sure it is like everything else. You get desensitized after a while. Heather told me that Ross Miniken found her first. I hadn't realized he was involved at all."

"Yeah, he went over there to help when Heather couldn't get her to come to the door. They were together when they found her." Conrad tested his chicken with a small bite.

"I don't know what to make of Ross. I've spoken to him several times and each time I come away with a different feeling. Arlene Emery doesn't like him at all and I can see that. He's a bit haughty and high-handed, but then he'll display concern for the town and act as though he really wants to be a part of the local life. I don't know what to think about him."

"I interviewed him today and I've got Tabor looking into his background. Something's fishy with that guy.

He doesn't want to talk about himself at all but he does act like we are all simpletons." Conrad sniffed the rice on his fork before tasting it.

"Regina really hasn't made any friends in town either. The merchants downtown say she always has her hand out asking for favors. I'm hoping that is just while she's struggling to open. Maybe once she is settled, she will start giving back."

"She wasn't very cooperative either. Brook has worked for her for a couple of years and she seems to know nothing about her. The parents will be here in the morning and I'm hoping they can tell me something about this strange working arrangement."

"I guess you'll have a busy weekend!"

"Not really. After I talk to the parents, there isn't much I can do until Alice gives me some direction."

"I'm planning to take it easy. My proposed budget for next year is done and I am free now to concentrate on the Thanksgiving dinner. Jason Marks sent me some ideas to look over and we are going to start advertising it right after Labor Day."

"The giant potluck?" Conrad chuckled. "Is Saucy going to dress up as a turkey?"

Cora's eyebrows lifted in a smile as if she was considering the idea. "Actually, this giant potluck is just made for people like Saucy. No one should be alone on the holidays." Saucy's sister, June, had been his only family and she was now in a nursing home.

"No offense, but I'm going for the food. I plan to have a spoonful of everything there."

Cora Mae smiled. "That sounds like a good plan!"

Chapter 17

Peggy walked out of the storage room and looked out the front window of the store. Saturdays were usually their busiest day, but it had been very quiet so far. With clouds rolling in suggesting rain, business may not pick up. "I think I'm going to take Sully out for his walk now before it rains. Is Fennel Street peaceful?"

Arlene looked up from the cutting table and huffed. "Pretty quiet out there today. No giant trucks unloading so far. I saw Regina leave a few minutes ago, but I assume the girls are working."

"I guess things are just business as usual over there." Peggy shook her head in confusion as she squatted down to hook the leash to Sully's harness. "I can't figure them out."

"I'm going to get started on a cross-stitch display

from your pattern of the Salty Shipper sign. It should work up really quickly, and we'll have an example to show the girls at our Tuesday Tea." Arlene cut a rectangle from a sheet of colonial blue Aida cloth. "The Carom Seed Craft Corner sign is a bit more complex."

"How many responses have you received from the email invitation so far?" Peggy pulled the door open so Sully could walk out.

"Only four so far, but I'm sure Cora Mae will stop in if she can."

"We'll be back in a few minutes." Peggy pulled the door shut and turned Sully towards Paprika Parkway. The sky was darkening so she didn't want to get more than a block away from the store. Turning at the drugstore, she crossed the street and walked slowly towards the bakery, loitering a little near the opening of the Sassafras store. Sully took advantage of her delay to sniff the area thoroughly and Peggy realized that she couldn't stop in to say hello with a dog. She should have planned this better.

"Good morning, Peggy." Kim opened the door with a box in her hands.

"Good morning. How are you?" Sully looked up as if he was prepared to answer.

"Good. It looks like rain." Kim opened the passenger side door of her car parked in front of the store and tossed the box in the front seat.

"It does. That's why we didn't want to walk very far."

"Do you want to come in? Regina is gone and probably won't be back for a while. Sully can come, too!" Kim pulled the door open and stood to the side as Peggy led Sully inside. The girls were scattered around in different corners on separate projects, but most were staring intently at their phones. "We've gotten a little more done since you were here, but we still need the handyman to come back. He's going to build a couple of dressing rooms in the back."

"Oh, I didn't think about that! Yes, you will need dressing rooms. Does Sassafras carry children's clothing at all?" Peggy pulled Sully close to her leg. She was afraid he might get into something he shouldn't.

"We don't. Just women's clothing, but the stores do tailor their orders to fit their local demand. I know not all the stores carry the same thing."

"Interesting." Peggy followed Kim to the cash wrap counter where Missy was stocking the counter space.

"Hi, Peggy! Who's your buddy?" Missy peered over the counter as Sully gazed up at her with excitement. He loved meeting new people.

"This is Sully. We were out for our short morning walk and ran into Kim. How are things this morning? Everything going okay?"

Missy walked around the counter and crouched

down to pet Sully. Looking over her shoulder first, Missy lowered her voice. "It's okay, I guess. Things are kinda weird right now. No one wants to talk about it, but I'm ready to get out of here, so I'm trying to get the work done as fast as possible."

Peggy hadn't thought of that. Maybe everyone was hard at work just to finish so they would be able to leave. "I know it's got to be shocking, especially when you're young. Young people don't die every day. It's so unexpected and final."

"It's even more creepy that it's not the first time. There was another girl that died on one of these trips. I didn't know her, but I heard about it. She was hit by a car, but still.... It's not normal, and I already told my boyfriend that this is the last one I'm going to do. If I get fired for it, I'll just have to find another job."

"That's horrible. I'm so sorry to hear that. How much longer do you think it will take?" Peggy looked around the room and thought it looked pretty close to complete. The clothing racks had been put together and some had clothes already hanging on them.

"At least another week." Missy stood up. "I don't know if I can take it."

"Do you go home on Sundays?"

"No. We have the day off, but it's too far for me. I usually just take it easy, but I might come in here and work a little to speed this up."

"Have you been to Paxton? There is more shopping over there and there are things to do at the lake if everybody wanted to get together and do something." Peggy had little experience entertaining tourists, but she had heard Arlene make these suggestions to visitors in her shop who came from out of town.

"We did go to Paxton the first weekend we were here, but just to look around. In the beginning we tried to be a friend group, but it just didn't work. I mean, everybody was okay, but we just didn't...."

"I understand. Different personalities." Peggy always envied Arlene's easy interactions with the public. Peggy had to work on that.

"Yeah. I get along okay with all of them. Eden talks to me the most, but she's a little dark." Missy raised an eyebrow. "She really didn't like Brook, but Brook was kinda perky. It could get on your nerves. Kim's a little bossy, but she's a hard worker, and Heather is devious. I stay away from her. I think she has a mean streak."

"It's difficult to bond as a team if you're all in competition."

"Exactly." Missy nodded and glanced at the door when Heather walked in with a coffee cup from the Fennel Street Bakery in her hand. "That's a perfect example. Heather went next door for coffee and didn't even tell anyone or offer to get them anything. Everyone's quit trying to be a team."

"That's a shame." Although Missy hadn't mentioned Regina, Peggy wondered how they felt about the boss.

Missy walked back around the counter. "I think Brook's parents are here now. Regina was going over to the inn to meet them and take them to the police station. I hope they don't come over here. I don't know what to say to them."

"I know it feels awkward, but you just tell them that everyone is devastated for them. That stuff never gets easy."

Missy lowered her eyes and shrugged.

Peggy knew she had overstayed her welcome, but had to try a direct approach. "What do you think happened to Brook?"

"I don't have any idea. Regina said she wasn't hurt or murdered, so I guess she just had a heart attack or something. No clue."

"Hmm, I guess the police will figure it out. It looks like Regina is going to stay here and open the store, but I hope your part wraps up soon, so you can go home."

"Thanks, Peggy."

"We've got to get back. Come over if you get a break. Arlene can set you up with a new craft to keep you busy tomorrow on your day off!"

Missy laughed as she waved goodbye.

Harvey "Saucy" Salzman drove his truck carefully down the rutted drive to Mavis Bell's greenhouse. He had already been to Herman Latley's farm and picked up a travel cage for the rooster. Now he had to convince one of them to take a ride.

"Hey, Saucy!" Mavis waved from the side of the chicken coop. "I'm over here."

"When are you going to get a load of gravel for that driveway, Mavis? I'm going to lose a tooth one of these days!"

Mavis laughed and gave him a dismissive wave. "It's on my list, but since I just walk across the street to get here, it slips my mind until we get a big rain."

"Well, we might just get that today, so we better get moving. I got a cage from Herman in the back of the truck. Did you decide on which rooster you want me to take to Herman's farm?"

"I've never had a problem deciding, Saucy. It's always been you that keeps trying to change my mind. I want to keep Glen."

Saucy shook his head in disappointment. Glen was a nice bird, but Hank was the better rooster. He had failed to convince Mavis of the importance of that job.

"Okay, if that's what you want. I'll get the cage."

Mavis went into her office and pulled a slice of watermelon from her refrigerator. After Saucy set the cage on the ground and wrangled the door open, he went to grab Hank Williams. When he returned with the protesting bird, Mavis tossed the watermelon into the cage and Hank hopped inside. It was his special weakness.

"I went to dinner with that train guy I told you about. You know that guy that put the ad in the paper?"

"Oh, yeah. How did that go? Is he going to buy your train set?"

"He made me an offer, but I haven't made up my mind. What he really wants is yours." Saucy pointed at her.

"Mine? Mine isn't for sale."

"I told him about it and I was right. It's worth a pretty penny. I thought you should know."

"It's just an old-fashioned train that Clarence gave the kids. I'm not sure if his parents bought it for him when he was a child or if it was already in the family before that, but it's old." Clarence Farrell had been Mavis' first husband and was the father of her children. Clarence and Saucy had been friends in those early years.

"He told me that it sounds like a ten thousand dollar set! I haven't seen it in years, but I told him what I could remember. He'd like to see it."

"I drag it out at Christmas and put it around the tree for the grandkids. They think it's the Polar Express." Mavis chuckled.

Saucy rolled his eyes. "You should really talk to this guy. It may be worth thousands more."

Mavis shook her head. "If it's worth something now, it will be worth something later. The grandkids can sell it if they need to, but I'm not interested."

"At least let him appraise it. Show it to him and see what he says. What can that hurt?" Saucy dug around in his pocket and pulled out a business card. "His number is on there and he's staying at the Nutmeg Inn for another week."

"I'll think about it."

Chapter 18

Conrad called the number Regina had given him for her brother, Garrett Adkins. After speaking briefly with Garrett's wife, he settled back in his desk chair to wait for him to come to the phone.

"This is Garrett."

"Mr. Adkins. This is Chief Harris with the Spicetown Police Department. Your sister, Regina, gave me your number and I'd like to ask you a few questions about Brook Calvert."

"Yes, Regina told me what happened. I was shocked to hear about it. As far as I knew, Brook was healthy. I don't know that I can be of any help."

"Tell me about her time with you. Regina said she worked for you initially?"

"Yes. She worked in my office, administrative stuff

mostly. She handled our phones and appointments, that type of thing."

"What type of work do you do?"

"Financial Planning," Garrett said. "Insurance, annuities, investments, you know."

"So, what caused the change?" Conrad leaned forward across his desk for his notepad. "Why did she become an employee of Regina's?"

"I just thought it might be a better fit for her. She thought so, too."

Conrad paused and tapped his pen on the notepad. He wasn't buying it. "I was under the impression there was another reason. Can you elaborate a little?"

After a long pause, Garrett said, "What did Regina say?"

Conrad smiled. He was right and he wasn't going to help him out of his lie. "Brook's parents are in town now to offer their help. Have you met them?"

"Uh, no. I mean Brook spoke of them often, but we've never met."

Seed planted. Conrad moved in again. "I'd like to hear your side of what transpired when Brook moved from your employ to Regina's."

"My wife wanted her gone." Garrett blew air against the receiver and lowered his voice. "She thought there was something going on between us and she wanted Brook gone. I didn't want to fire her, so I asked

Regina if she had something for her."

"Was there something going on?" Conrad leaned back and quietly sighed. It was an often-told tale.

"No! My wife is overly jealous. I couldn't reason with her."

"Uh huh." Conrad's chair squeaked when he leaned forward.

"She has trust issues."

"Hmm."

"We had a rough patch a few years ago and she's never really moved past it."

Conrad translated that. "You cheated on her with an employee before?" Conrad didn't want to do this dance.

"Yeah, but that was different."

Of course it was. "Tell me what you know about Brook."

"She was a bright girl. She always showed up on time and tried really hard to please. Everyone liked her. She lived at home with her parents back then and was taking some classes online to get an associate's degree in something, but she didn't really have any firm plans for the future."

"Any relationships that you know of? Did she have a boyfriend or mention girlfriends?"

"No, not to me. We didn't chat about personal stuff."

"And after she switched over to work for Regina, did you hear from her?"

"No. Regina said she was working out fine and I never gave it another thought."

"Okay," Conrad's shoulders slumped. "If you think of anything that might be relevant, please give me a call. Thank you for your time."

Saucy walked around to the back of his pickup and looked at Hank Williams. "I'm sorry about this, big boy. I tried to fight for you to stay, but you really shouldn't have chased Mavis around and pecked her ankles." Hank turned his head. "You wait here and I'll be right back."

Saucy wandered slowly up to one of the barns on the Latley Farm and looked around for someone, but Herman found him first.

"Hey, Saucy. Did you bring me a new bird?"

"I sure did. He's one of my favorites, but Mavis didn't feel like he was a good fit for her flock."

"They all have their own personalities!"

"Yeah, they do. She's just getting started, a little green, you know. She didn't intend to have a rooster and she ended up with two."

"Oh, I understand. You learn as you go and a good rooster can be hard to handle." Herman followed Saucy around to the bed of his truck.

"This is Hank Williams. Mavis got him when Eli Buford gave her some chicks this spring, so he's young. I figured he might be a Blue Plymouth Rock, but he gave Mavis a mixed group of chicks." Hank had a black body with white around his neck and head. Exuding confidence, he gave Herman his best pose as he looked him up and down.

"He's a good-looking boy. I'm sure he'll do fine out here. Let me grab him." Herman lifted the crate from the pickup and carried him up near the back door of his house as Saucy followed. Rapping his knuckles on the screen door, he called out to his wife. "Hey, Glory. Come out here and meet Hank Williams!"

Saucy chuckled as Gloria Latley looked through the top glass of the door. "Hi, Gloria."

"Hi, Saucy. What a beautiful boy he is! I think you named him well."

"It wasn't just me. He's Mavis Bell's boy, but he pecked her one time too many."

Gloria laughed. "Roosters can get bossy. You have to pick them up the minute they get feisty and walk around with them for a while. I take a whole stroll around the property holding them and if you do that every time they try to push you around, they'll learn that you're the real boss."

"Glory is the chicken whisperer." Herman chuckled.

"Well, I see people get mad and kick at them or yell at them. That's no good at all. You have to stroke their neck and talk real calm to them. They'll respect you. They'll figure out that they can't pick you up, so you must be the boss."

Saucy nodded. He had kicked at a few when he was a boy, too. "I'll pass your advice on to Mavis. She still has one rooster, but he's very tame. That's why she wanted to keep him. I'm sure there will be more roosters in her future though."

"Yep, I'm sure another will turn up later on." Herman poked his finger in the cage and Hank stabbed his beak at it. "I think I'll put him in the pen next to Bertha's flock and let them get acquainted before I mix him in."

Gloria nodded as Herman carried Hank Williams around the side of the house. "Saucy, did you hear about the dead girl in town? Was she anybody you knew?" Gloria put her hand on her hip and frowned.

"Brook, yeah, I'd met her. She's one of the girls that just came to help set up the new clothing store downtown. There's a group of them, but they aren't staying. They were just going to be here for a few weeks."

"Such a shame. Herman met her the night before she died. He said she was a nice girl, real young, too."

"Yes, she was. I saw Herman the morning they found her. He was doing some work at their store. I didn't realize he'd been there before."

"Nope, not there. He met her over at that rental house. He does some pickup work for Red Pepper Realty and her A/C was out. Clyde called him the night before and he went over there."

"The night before she was found?" Saucy's heart raced. "Was she all right when he was there?"

"Oh, yeah. He said they just chatted while he worked. She seemed real sweet."

"Yes, she did. You need to tell Herman to call the chief and let him know though. He may be the last person to see her alive and I'm sure Chief Harris would want to know about it."

"Okay, I'll tell him. You take care, Saucy, and tell your sister, June, that I said hello."

"I will. Thank you, Gloria." Saucy climbed in his truck and looked at his phone. He should call someone, but it was late afternoon on a Saturday. Maybe he'd drive by the police station and see if the chief was there. This couldn't wait until Monday and Clyde Newman might have been over there, too. He needed to find the chief.

Chapter 19

"Okay, I can't stand it." Peggy put her hands on her hips and flashed Arlene a guilty look. "I've got to go over there." They had both been watching the window all morning, hoping Regina would have an errand to run and Peggy could slip over for a simple hello.

"What excuse are you going to use to visit? We don't have any more food to take." Arlene looked around the store. "I can't think of anything we have that they would need."

Peggy's eyes opened wide as her frown disappeared. "Herman! Herman Latley is back over there working and I can say I need to talk to him. I can ask him to put up another shelf for us on the shipping side. Don't you think we could use another one over there?"

"It's going to cost you." Arlene smiled. "Your

curiosity could get expensive."

"You're right, but I can justify it. Mildred said she was thinking about putting some of her quilts on sale for consignment and we don't have room over there for that right now. I can tell her tomorrow when she comes to the knitting group that we are having an extra shelf built just for her!"

"That's a way to pressure her." Arlene laughed. "She says stuff like that all the time and then doesn't follow through."

"Exactly! Two birds with one stone!" Peggy huffed and started for the door.

"How much is that stone going to cost you?" Arlene's eyebrows raised.

Peggy paused with her hand on the doorknob. "Oh, I don't know. I can always decline if the price is too much, I guess. Go ahead and call in our lunch order and I'll pick them up at Dorothy's on my way back."

Arlene nodded as the bells jingled when Peggy flew out of the door.

Dodging parked cars, Peggy crisscrossed Fennel Street until she could peer inside the front door to Sassafras. She could see the construction of the dressing room was in full swing, but she didn't see Herman Latley anywhere. Her mission remained the same.

"Hello, everyone. I hope you don't mind if I stop in to speak to Herman for just a second. I saw he was working over here today and I promise I won't stay." Peggy's words rushed out to keep anyone from objecting and it worked.

"Hi, Peggy. Herman is out back in the alley cutting some boards. I'm sure he'll be right back." Kim answered because she was the only person not scrolling through her phone.

Regina nodded. "Hi, Peg. Yeah, he'll be right in. Are you having some work done, too?"

"Herman put up some shelves for me when the shipping store opened, but I need a few more. I thought I'd let him know while he was here. It's just a small job, but maybe he can work me in sometime during the next few weeks."

"Sure! That's no problem. He'll be done here in a few days. I've got to run upstairs. Make yourself comfortable." Regina carried a box up the stairs and looked down at Eden. "Please put your phone away and finish stocking that case."

Eden slipped her phone in her back pocket and grabbed a small box from the floor to place on the counter. Peggy watched as she pulled out crinkly bags and tiny boxes, stacking them across the top of the counter to decide how to arrange them.

"Oh, you have jewelry?" Peggy walked closer to the counter as Eden pulled out a long necklace from its plastic pouch.

"Yes, just a few pieces. We use some as accessories on the mannequins, but the rest we keep in this glass case. We usually have a few scarves and belts, too."

"How nice!" Peggy reached out to turn the pendant over as it dangled from Eden's hand. "Arlene loves giraffes! I may have to come back when you open and pick that up for her birthday."

Eden smiled. "Our stuff is a little quirky sometimes, but that's what makes it fun." Pushing her hair back over her ear, she turned her head sideways. "See these little lady bugs? I got these at my store last year and I just love them."

Peggy was dazzled by Eden's smile. It was the first time she'd seen her do anything other than sulk since she arrived. "It's so much better to shop when you can see the item you're buying. I'm not a big fan of shopping online, but small towns don't have a lot of local choices."

"You should come back later and I'll have everything unwrapped. Then you can get a sneak peek before the rest of the town."

Peggy chuckled. "I will definitely do that!"

"What promises are you making?" Regina said to Eden as she walked down the stairway.

Regina's sideways smirk might have been in teasing, but Peggy wasn't going to stick around and find out. "I'm going to step out back if that's okay and see if I can grab a quick word with Herman before I run to the cafe to pick up lunch. I'm looking forward to seeing all of your great merchandise soon!"

Not waiting for a reply, Peggy cut through the storage room, waving to Missy as she slipped out the back door. Herman had a plastic saw horse set up and his saw was making too much noise for him to realize he had company. Peggy moved slowly into his line of vision to avoid scaring him into losing a finger.

Herman did jump a little when he realized her movement, but he shut off his circular saw, lifted his safety glasses up to the top of his head and stepped back as the motor whined to a stop.

"Hi, Herman. I'm sorry to interrupt you. I just saw you were working over here and stopped over to chat with you about a couple of extra shelves I'll be needing at the shipping store. It's not urgent. I just wanted you to put me on your list."

"Sure, Peg. I can do that next week if you want. Maybe Wednesday, if that would be all right. I'm running a little behind on this job, so I'm not certain when I'll be free. I got a late start this morning."

"This is your second job today!"

"No. I had to talk to the chief this morning about the girl that died. He wanted me to stop by first thing." Herman lowered his voice. "Did you know the girl that died? Brook?"

"I did. She was sweet and so young. We were all

shocked. I still don't know what caused her death. She seemed fine earlier in the day."

"I said the same thing! I went over to that house she was staying at and worked on her A/C. The chief said I must have been the last person that saw her before.... Well, you know."

"Oh! You saw her that night?"

Herman nodded. "She just sat at the counter in the kitchen eating a piece of pie and talking to me while I worked. I had to replace the thermostat and it's right around the corner."

"Wow!" Peggy shook her head. "I can't imagine what happened to her."

"The chief said she probably died a couple of hours after I left and she was perfectly fine when I was there. We talked about her job and she said she was a little homesick. I think she was ready for this trip to be over. She said it was probably going to last another two weeks and she wanted to get back home before her niece went back to school, so she could take her to the zoo."

"I don't think the girls in there were very friendly to her." Peggy grimaced as she pointed at the back door. "That probably made the job a little more difficult for her, especially since she was the lead worker."

"Yeah, nobody likes the boss." Herman chuckled. "The chief said her parents are in town. I can't imagine what they're going through right now."

"It doesn't seem to have affected the rest of the group much. They went right back to work the day she was found. I think I would have given the idea of opening a business in this town a second thought." Peggy held her hands up. "Not that Spicetown is a dangerous place, but they don't know that."

"That's true. I would have probably been scared off, too. I guess we're lucky that they weren't."

Peggy hummed. She wasn't sure of that yet. "Listen, I'll get going and let you get back to work. Just let me know when you've got time for me and we'll hash out the details later."

"Sure thing, Peggy. Thanks."

Peggy waved goodbye as she walked through the open storage room door. Missy was no longer working back there, so she walked back into the main lobby of the store. Glancing around, Kim was the only one that registered her return because the others were back to looking at their phones. Peggy walked over to the hanging clothes rack.

"Have a seat!" Kim pointed to a chair nearby. "You can move Heather's purse out of the way."

Peggy looked down at Heather's open bag with a pink rhinestone phone in the side pocket and a package of cheese puffs tossed on top, but then realized their lunches were probably getting cold. "That's okay. I'm going to head back across the street. I need to pick up our lunch orders and get back to the store."

"Well, come back any time. You're always welcome."

"Thank you! I just might do that. I am really enjoying watching this store come to life." Peggy smiled and had to admit to herself that having a sneak peek at their progress was giving her inner nosy neighbor some satisfaction.

"I'm glad you're enjoying it." Kim chuckled. "To me sometimes it feels like I'm watching grass grow instead."

Chapter 20

Peggy rushed across the street and charged into the Caraway Cafe with relief that her order was not sitting on the counter yet. She waved to Dorothy, who was delivering orders to Chief Harris and Cora Mae, who sat at their usual table in the large front window.

Peggy saw the chief point his fork at her and say something to Cora, who spun around in her chair. "Hi, Peggy. Come join us!"

Peggy shook her head feeling guilty for disrupting their meal. She never stayed to chat after the food arrived. "I'm just waiting for my orders."

"They'll be up in a minute." Dorothy waved her to come closer, so Peggy walked over to their table.

"Have a seat. You can wait with us until it's ready." Cora pointed to the chair on the side of the table.

"No, I don't want to bother you while you're eating."

Peggy took a step backwards, but then came back and held up her finger. "Just a quick reminder. Did you get Arlene's email about the knitting group starting back up? The first meeting is tomorrow."

"I did!" Cora Mae stirred her tea. "I can't be there at two o'clock, because Amanda has me booked, but I may stop in once my appointment is over. It depends on how late it is. I'm anxious to see everyone again."

"Have a seat." Conrad frowned at Peggy and pointed to the chair, so she lowered herself to the edge of the chair as Dorothy walked away to get another order.

"Thank you. I was just across the street checking on the Sassafras girls. Herman Latley is over there working and I wanted to grab him before he got too booked up. I need a little help at The Salty Shipper." Peggy looked over her shoulder at the order counter again. "Herman said he talked to you this morning."

Conrad nodded.

"He said he may have been the last person to see Brook alive."

"That's right. I didn't know he'd been by her house until Saucy told me. I wanted to see what time he was there because we don't have an exact time of death yet."

"What time estimate are you using?" Cora Mae cut her sandwich in half and picked one up.

"About eight o'clock that night." Conrad shrugged his shoulders and huffed. "Give or take a couple of hours. Alice is still working on it."

"Do you have any idea what caused the death?" Peggy looked at Cora Mae because she was afraid Conrad would be scowling at her question, but he wasn't.

"Not yet. We should hear something soon though. Her parents are really putting on the pressure. I think they'll put a rush on things because they don't want it to become a media event." Conrad shuddered. "Young people dying for no reason is a shock to everyone in the community, even if they don't know the victim."

"As they should be! It's such a tragedy," Cora said with a wave of her salad fork.

"Do they run tests on everything in the house, too? Or is it just testing on her?" Peggy couldn't fathom how they could determine what made someone's heart stop by looking at a dead body.

"They test anything we bring them, but only after they figure out what the cause could be. It's a needle in a haystack otherwise."

"Peggy, you're up!" Dorothy called out from the checkout counter and Peggy jumped from her chair.

"Well, my lunches are ready so I'll leave you both in peace now. Enjoy your lunch and I hope to see you tomorrow, Cora."

Peggy walked up to the door of the Carom Seed Craft Corner and waited for Arlene to open the door. She couldn't turn the doorknob with two drinks and two lunch containers in her hand. Arlene was usually watching for her, but her timing was a bit off since she'd left early to visit Sassafras.

Bending forward she looked between the lettering on the glass door to peer inside, but Arlene wasn't there. Peggy looked around the street and then walked over to door of The Salty Shipper and found her. Arlene was waiting on a customer who was shipping a package, so she'd have to catch the door as the customer left.

"Hi, Mrs. Cochran." Jason Marks strolled down the sidewalk with a curious look. "Do you need some help?"

"Hi, Jason. I'm just waiting on Arlene. She's got a customer and I'm going to grab the door when he leaves. Are you on your lunch break?"

"Yeah, I don't really know what to do with myself." Jason chuckled. "Let me get the door for you."

"Oh, if you would, I'd rather go in the craft side."

"Sure." Jason walked over and pushed the door in but it didn't want to stay, so he walked inside and held the door open for Peggy. "You know, I'm not sure I've ever been in here."

Peggy sat the food on the checkout counter just as Sully sounded a gruff welcome bark.

"Who is this?" Jason walked over slowly to Sully's dog bed and turned back to look at Peggy for reassurance.

"Oh, that's Sully. You haven't met him before? We walk around downtown all the time." Peggy thought everyone had met him by now. "I guess you wouldn't because Dorothy would never let me bring him inside the Caraway Cafe."

Jason laughed and squatted down in front of Sully, waiting for his next move.

"He's friendly. Probably too friendly."

Jason held out his hand and Sully walked right into a free ear rub. "No, I'm sure Dorothy wouldn't let him in, and I didn't get out much when I worked at the Caraway. That's why I don't know what to do with myself having a lunch hour. An hour! It does not take an hour to eat. I was just pacing around waiting to catch the mayor when she leaves. I saw her through the window eating lunch with the chief and I didn't want to interrupt, but I have news for her about the Thanksgiving dinner."

"Are you working with her on that? It sounds like it will be a fun day. I'm just glad it won't be an event she'll put me to work on. I can't cook a lick!"

Jason chuckled. "Yeah, I'm sure Dorothy is a little worried about how big her investment will be, but we really are trying to make it a simple potluck for everyone. That's what I wanted to tell her. The bank has agreed to buy all the meat if she'll show them as a sponsor of the event. I think that will be a huge relief to her. Now all she has to do is organize it."

"I think she'll love that!" Peggy nodded.

"I hope so. Are you working the costumes for the next play?"

"Yes, Cora said it's going to be a small Christmas production called 'Welcome to Virginia'. It only has 6 people in it with no costume changes, so I am feeling blessed."

Jason laughed. "That doesn't sound like Christmas, but I'm sure the mayor knows what she's doing."

"Do you like your job at the bank?" Peggy's eyes narrowed in thought. Jason was meant for bigger things than cooking lunch at the Caraway Cafe, but the bank didn't entirely seem the right spot either. "Is it something you see yourself doing long term?"

"Did the mayor tell you to ask me that?" Jason gave a sly smile. "She's asked me the same thing more than once."

"No, not at all. I just have a hard time seeing you there."

"You think I should have stayed at the cafe?" Jason's head dropped and he turned back to Sully's demands for a tummy rub.

"No. I don't think that. I think you did the right thing leaving when you did, but I'll deny I said that if you tell Dorothy."

Jason smiled.

"I just see you as doing something more interactive,

like being a real estate tycoon or a director of some big project. I don't know." Peggy shrugged. "Maybe running for election! You would be great at all that campaigning and speech-ifying stuff. Don't you think? I could see you doing that."

Jason patted Sully's head and stood up. "I don't know about all that, but I'm okay where I am right now. I did think about real estate, but Red Pepper Realty seems to have that handled for now. I want to do something that makes a difference. I'll just have to try a few things to find out where the right place is for me, I guess."

"I'm sure you'll know it when you see it," Peggy said as Jason walked to the door. "Speaking of real estate, do you know who bought Jacob Hart's building over there?" Peggy pointed toward Clove Street. "I know Ross Miniken rented it, but I haven't had a chance to ask him who leased it to him."

"Well, it wasn't a person. It was a real estate investment trust. They call it a REIT and it's a company that buys up income-producing properties. You can invest in them like a mutual fund and you get a monthly dividend check when all the properties pay their rent."

"Interesting! I've never heard of that. How did Jacob's son find that kind of buyer?"

"I think Ross steered them to Jeremiah. He probably knows them since he does financial planning for people. I'm sure he's helped people invest in REITs when he was managing their money. He could have pitched the idea to the company himself and they contacted Jeremiah with an offer. You can't beat having a guaranteed renter that you already know!"

"Like getting a friend to buy the building so he could rent from them?" Peggy's smirk slipped out before she could catch it. "Something about that feels a little sneaky to me."

"Oh, it's perfectly legal. They are good investments."

"You're so smart!" Peggy grinned at Jason as he pulled the door open. "Maybe you'll run the bank someday!"

Jason blushed. "Thanks. I'll see you later."

Chapter 21

Mavis Bell had her egg apron full and grabbed a basket to handle the overflow of eggs she'd received from her chickens, so she didn't even turn around when she heard a vehicle bouncing down the road to her greenhouse. Saucy usually stopped by in the late afternoon just to talk to her chickens and make sure she was managing the coop properly.

His oversight had come in handy, but she had read everything in print on this venture before she began. Still, having his support had made the journey less lonely since her son had taken a full-time job in Paxton and Saucy seemed to benefit from his role as well. Everyone needed to have a purpose.

"Hey, Mavis. You won't believe who I just saw!"

Mavis raised her eyebrows and pretended to think

hard about her answer. "Hmm, Hank Williams?"

Saucy's shoulders dropped as he admitted defeat. "Okay, so you're not surprised, but I needed to make sure he didn't feel abandoned. Herman said he had to be caged separately for a week and he's in there all alone. All the other chickens are next to him, but he can't make friends that way."

"He's in a cage for a week?" Mavis scowled. She expected Hank would be running free and happy in a large flock.

"It's a pen, really. He's got lots of room, but he's all alone. Herman said he's trying to peck everybody through the wire, so he needs to get acclimated slowly. They'll give him his own flock next week and he'll get to be in charge again."

"Oh, well that's okay, I guess. Did he give you a peck hello?" Mavis chuckled. Hank Williams wasn't any nicer to Saucy than he was to her, but it seemed to bother Saucy less.

"I don't know about that, but he looked fine. Gloria told me how to train bossy roosters and Herman says she'll have Hank in line real soon. I can't wait to see that!"

"Do you see all these eggs I have?" Mavis pointed to her pockets and held up her basket. "What am I going to do with all of these? The girls are so happy Hank is gone that they've overdone themselves. I can't let these all go to waste."

"Sell them!" Saucy slapped his legs against his thighs.

"I don't have my registration yet. They have to do an inspection and then there's a license or a permit. Something or other. I can't remember all the details, but it's a lot!"

"Okay," Saucy kicked the wood shavings that had been tracked from the chicken pen into the grass. "Give them away. If your friends offer you a donation, then it's not the same as selling."

"Is that legal advice? Are you going to law school online and didn't tell me?" Mavis laughed. "Maybe the better question is, are you going to bail me out of jail when the egg police come?"

Saucy rolled his eyes and shook his head, but he couldn't hide his smile. "I've got your back. You know, tomorrow is Peggy's knittin' group meeting and I bet you could unload all of them in one trip up there. I saw she had a sign on the door about it. Do you need help to get them up there?"

They both turned their head when they heard the hum of an engine slowly navigating Mavis' bumpy driveway to the greenhouse. "Who could that be?"

Saucy squinted his eyes. "I don't recognize the car. Maybe someone's lost."

"Fancy car." Mavis smirked. It must be a city

person who was trying to find adventure on a country road.

"That looks like Mr. Abbott." Saucy gave a tentative wave as the car stopped next to his truck. "He's the train guy." Saucy saw Mavis give him a harsh side-eyed glance. "I didn't tell him where you lived. I promise, I just told him I would pass his phone number to you so you could contact him if you were interested in a train appraisal. That's all.

"Mr. Abbott?" Saucy squinted to see the man getting out of the black sedan.

"Hello, Mr. Salzman." Mr. Abbott began walking toward the chicken coop with a forced smile. "Is this Mrs. Bell, by any chance?"

Saucy glanced at Mavis, afraid to confirm the question.

"I'm Mavis Bell." Mavis swiped her hands together to dust off the dirt. "How can I help you?"

"The question is how can I help you." Mr. Abbott stopped in front of Mavis and stretched out his hand. "I'm Harold Abbott and I collect trains."

Mavis shook his hand without any visible reaction to his attempt at humor. She did not appreciate uninvited guests.

Saucy chuckled nervously. "I told her about our meeting and gave her your number, but I don't think she's looking to sell."

"I understand, but I am able to at least offer an appraisal. Even if you aren't interested in selling it, you could benefit knowing it's value. Before I leave town, I just wanted to offer my services, free of charge."

Mavis scowled. "So, you drove out here to offer your services free to a total stranger. What's in it for you?"

Mr. Abbott smiled. "My dear lady, I love trains. I'm excited to see what you have and I'll enjoy it, even if you aren't interested in selling. I'm also hoping that if you ever change your mind, I will be the person you call first."

"An appraisal won't sway me, Mr. Abbott. That set is a family heirloom and I plan to pass it down to my children and grandchildren, no matter the value. There's no reason for either of us to waste our time on an appraisal."

Mr. Abbott shrugged. "I understand, but I am here." He held his arms open. "And I would really enjoy seeing it. Could you consider letting me take a look?"

Saucy relaxed. "I wouldn't mind seeing it again myself, Mavis. It's been years."

Mavis did not waiver. "I'm sorry you came all this way, Mr. Abbott, but I'm not interested and I've got work to do here. I'm sure you'll find other train sets on your travels."

Mr. Abbott frowned. "I don't understand--."

Mavis interrupted him. "How much room for

interpretation did I leave?"

"Sorry, Mr. Abbott." Saucy grabbed his arm and turned him back toward his car. "I'll keep your number and I'll share it with anyone I hear of that might have something you would be interested in. I probably shouldn't have mentioned Mavis without asking her first. I wasn't thinking about her family. I know her kids love seeing it at Christmas. I'm sure you understand."

Mavis turned her back to the men as they walked to the car and began placing her eggs into egg cartons. She could use an afternoon break tomorrow. She might just make a visit to town after lunch and drop in on the knitting group.

Long after Saucy had gone home, Mavis closed up her chickens and her greenhouse to walk back across the road to her home. Daniel was not coming home tonight. He had called to say he was staying on the couch at a friend's house in Paxton because he had an early report to work the next day. As she walked up her driveway, she saw her front screen door was ajar. A good wind could come along and pull it open, but for right now, it was just unlatched and resting against the door frame. She never used the front door unless company rang the bell, so she wondered if she had missed a visitor. She always came out the side door near the detached garage.

Walking up her porch steps, she looked inside the

screen door to see if a pamphlet had been left behind. There were occasionally sales representatives that would still visit, but that practice wasn't as common as it once was. Turning the knob, she was relieved to find her steel door was locked, but she gave it a hard shake just to be certain. Then it dawned on her. It was probably Mr. Abbott. He must have come to her home first before venturing across the road to the land.

She couldn't say why, but the man had given her an unsettled feeling from the moment he approached, and he was not someone she would ever invite into her home. Regardless, she had been honest with him. She did not want to know the value of the train set, and she did not plan to sell it. It was the only thing of value she had from her first husband, Clarence Farrell and it should go to their children.

She couldn't deny being a little spooked by the thought someone had been lurking around her home and decided to walk around the house before going inside. Her son, Daniel, had mentioned more than once that he worried about her out here all alone, which had made her laugh. She thought he said it because he was looking for free room and board, but maybe there was a mature concern blooming there. He had done a lot of growing up in the last couple of years.

Once around the side corner of the house, she was distracted by her Weigela bush that had become overgrown and misshapen. She should have pruned it once it had finished flowering, but it was too late in the summer for that now. This fall she planned to take some cuttings to propagate in her greenhouse and she looked deep into the bush for mature hardwood stems to harvest. It was just another experiment on her to-do list, and remembering her original purpose, she turned to walk across the back of her house.

Before she reached the corner near the garage, she saw the screen window to her laundry room had been violently slashed and then raised in the metal track. It was a calculated choice being away from sight by people on the road and the wood frame window appeared to be unlocked. The failed intruder wouldn't know it had been painted shut decades ago and Mavis had never bothered to remedy that, since the laundry room wasn't a place she spent much quality time. Now, this would be something else she would need to add to her to-do list.

Chapter 22

"Good morning, Chief." Roy Asher pushed away from the dispatch desk as Briscoe crawled into the dog bed under the counter. "The state crime stats are filed and Georgia brought muffins. They're in the break room."

"Thank you, Roy." Conrad glanced around the room as if he wasn't sure where he was.

"Hey, Chief." Eugene Tabor waved as he walked out of the break room with a muffin in his other hand.

"Any luck on your research?" Conrad glanced at the muffin in Tabor's hand and calculated the odds that he could resist them.

Eugene pulled his desk chair out and dropped his muffin on a napkin. "Well, I think I dug up more questions than answers."

"How so?" Conrad walked over to Eugene's desk.

"That Miniken guy." Eugene shook his head and huffed. "I don't think he's real."

"What? What do you mean?" Conrad hadn't asked for identification, but maybe he should have.

"I don't know exactly what he claims to be, but I thought he would leave some tracks. He should have had a prior business somewhere. Right? He said he retired. From what? I don't know."

"I thought someone told me he was a financial planner." Conrad frowned in an attempt to remember where he heard that. It was probably Cora Mae.

"I don't know if they're licensed or not, but they should at least be educated. He just doesn't exist." Tabor tossed his hands up in the air. "Anywhere."

"I believe they do require a license to practice. Did you find anyone named Miniken at all? Maybe he goes by his middle name or a nickname."

"No Miniken anywhere."

Conrad turned toward the hallway to his office muttering, "How can that be?"

"I'll keep digging!" Tabor yelled down the hallway.

Conrad logged into his computer thinking he might give it a try himself. Anyone can do a search and maybe Eugene Tabor's overly technical searches are missing the obvious. It could happen.

Mavis Bell entered the lobby of the police station with her arms wrapped around a large cardboard box. Her fingers barely reached around it and you could only see her eyes above the top edge, but she barreled toward the hallway. She had seen Conrad walking in the door with his police dog as she turned onto Paprika Parkway, so she knew he was in there.

"Hey! Hold up, Mavis." Roy Asher stood up and waved his pencil in the air. "Where are you going with that? You can't just go down there. Hold up!"

"I'm not speeding, Roy Asher, so you can't stop me." Officer Asher was famous for pulling people over for speeding and then giving them a lengthy speech on the dangers of reckless driving that eventually progressed to a warning. He didn't want to write a ticket because it required him to go to court in Paxton, but he needed to feel important to those in Spicetown. It was a tale frequently shared at morning coffee, because everyone had an Asher tale to tell. More than one person had asked for the ticket, just to get Roy to abbreviate the speech.

Mavis turned her back on Roy's stuttering and walked down the hallway toward the chief's office. The box prevented her from looking back, even if she wanted to.

Pausing at the doorway, she peeked inside to make certain he was alone and not on a phone call. "Morning,

Chief!"

Conrad stood up behind his desk to get a better look at who was behind the large box. "Good morning, Mavis."

Dropping the box in the visitor's chair across from his desk, she braced her knee against it to be certain it didn't tip over. "I need a favor."

Conrad peered into the box and saw a tangled mess of train cars before sitting down at his desk. "Does it have something to do with trains?"

"It does." Mavis nodded. "Would it be okay if I leave this box here for a few days?"

Conrad frowned. There was no specific reason he could come up with to say no, but he couldn't imagine why he had been chosen. "Why do you need to leave it anywhere?"

"I think someone is trying to steal it and it will take me a few days to make some suitable arrangements to prevent said theft, so I need a safe place." Mavis shrugged. "I don't know any place safer. Do you?"

"Now, wait." Conrad got up and lifted the box from the chair to place it on the floor by the window. "Sit down and tell me what's going on."

Mavis sighed. "Well, there's this guy. His name's Harold Abbott and he—."

"Yeah, I know him. He's obsessed with trains. The mayor had booked him for a show in the community center, but they couldn't work out the details, so she canceled it."

"That's him. Apparently, he advertised in the newspaper that he would give appraisals on train collections, and Saucy met him. During their talk, he mentioned my train set to the guy."

Conrad nodded. "Did he give you an appraisal?"

"No. I don't want one. I know it's valuable, but I don't want to sell it. He showed up on my land yesterday, trying to talk me into showing it to him. Then I get home and I find a screen on the back of my house has been cut open."

"Did you touch anything? You need to file a report on this."

Mavis tipped her hand dismissively at Conrad. "There's nothing to report. They couldn't get inside, but I need to do some reinforcing out there. Daniel's going to fix my screen this weekend and secure a few things for me. Until then, I just wanted to stash this in a safe place."

"I'd like to send someone out to check for fingerprints and we can increase patrols in the area. You can just push the box over in the corner there and it'll be fine for a few days." Conrad clasped his hands on his desktop and leaned forward on his elbows. "How did you leave things with Mr. Abbott?"

"With a firm, 'No thank you'. I'll feel better once

this guy leaves town. Something seems off with him."

"I don't disagree." Conrad smirked. He had said almost the same thing to Cora Mae. "I'll have Georgia run by sometime today and check out the window."

"Okay, gotta run." Mavis stood up and looked over at the train set box in the corner. "Let Georgia know I probably won't be home. I've got to run by the clinic and then this afternoon I'm bringing some eggs to town. I spend most of the day across the street at the greenhouse, anyway. Do you need any fresh eggs?"

"Yeah, I'd take a dozen. I'll ask Georgia when she calls in. She might want some, too."

Mavis nodded. "I'll stop back in later today. Thank you."

"That looks really nice, Arlene!" Peggy held the nearly completed cross-stitch replica of The Salty Shipper sign and looked at the stitching on the back before giving it back to Arlene. Her stitches were always so neat and clean. "How do you plan to finish it? Are you going to frame it or put it in a hoop?"

Arlene held it up in front of her. "I think I'll frame it, but I'll have to special order the size I want. I may make a second one to hang near the crossover doorway between the two shops. What do you think?"

"That's a great idea. I'm going to start one for the Carom Seed sign today. I think it would look nice on the door or maybe behind the cash register. I wish I could figure out a way to simplify the storefronts to a pattern that we could sell."

"Maybe cross stitch is the wrong method. It might be better to use embroidery. We could try tracing from the pictures of Sonjay's paintings. Maybe Mildred would offer us some suggestions on what type of stitches to use. She is so creative with making embroidery have great texture."

Peggy held up a finger and pointed at Arlene. "Then we could use the embroidery to make quilt blocks! We could make a whole quilt showing Spicetown shops."

"That would make an excellent group project. We could set it up in the community center and hold quilting circle meetings."

Peggy glanced at the clock. It was almost time for lunch. "Would you listen to us? One little cross-stitch picture of a store sign and we're planning to sew the entire town! Before we get carried away any further, I think we need to eat lunch. The girls will be showing up for group soon."

"Just think what we could have accomplished if we weren't hungry!" Arlene laughed. "I didn't hear back from Julia, but she might be out of town. I think the family goes on vacation about this time every year, before school starts."

"Cora said she has a meeting this afternoon, but she might stop in late if she can. Is everyone else coming?"

"Leona wasn't sure when I talked to her last, but Grace said she is coming. She's bringing treats that Imogene made, so I didn't make anything for the meeting. I have coffee made and a kettle of hot water if anyone wants tea."

"Wow! That's so nice of Grace." Peggy placed her palm over her heart. She had planned to run over to the bakery for cookies. "I was afraid she wouldn't come when I told her we couldn't hold it at her house anymore, but she seemed to understand."

"She likes to come into town in the summer, but I don't think she'll come during the colder months. I can't blame her. If I lived in a beautiful mansion like she does, I don't think I'd want to leave either."

"I feel bad that we didn't invite the Sassafras girls, but I don't think any of them do crafts." Peggy had looked for a reason to visit them this morning, but couldn't think of anything.

"Kim does a little, but I'm sure Regina wouldn't give her an hour off to come over. You need another good reason to go over there and get us a status report." Arlene knew the real reason for Peggy's angst as her deep thoughts creased her forehead. “Maybe you could get a Merchant’s Association application from Dorothy and take it over to show Regina. It would give you a reason to get in the door.”

“That’s true.” Peggy nodded. She would use that tomorrow morning. “Well, it’s still too hot to work with wool, so let’s get some thread kits out on the table in case someone needs a cool project and see what happens!”

“I’m on it!”

Chapter 23

Conrad abandoned his water pitcher in the break room and rushed down the hallway to his office when Roy Asher told him Coroner Alice Warner was on the phone. This call could close out his case or bust it wide open. He had a definite preference on which way he hoped it would go, but he was ready to handle either one.

"Hey, Alice. I hope you're calling me with some idea of which direction I go next, because I gotta tell you, right now I'm at a standstill."

Alice chuckled. "It doesn't sound like you've been standing still at all. It sounds like you've been running."

Conrad took a deep breath to slow his panting. "Oh, well, an old man needs a little exercise once in a while. Did you get the lab results?" Conrad dropped into his desk chair and grabbed his pen.

"I did."

Waiting a few seconds piqued his curiosity, but he knew Alice was just testing his patience and he wasn't going to give her that satisfaction. "Were the results a surprise to you?"

"Yes and no. I was thinking.... I'll be honest, I was hoping it was an allergic reaction because the autopsy results were not revealing. The young lady looked to be in excellent health with just a few signs of inflammation in a couple of areas."

"Yes, it's very sad to see a young life lost."

"The autopsy was a treat to me. You have no idea how many old, diseased or damaged bodies I get on a regular basis."

Conrad could hear the smile in Alice's words, but her words triggered a small gag reflex in him. He knew her comments were meant for that. If she couldn't poke him one way, she found another. "Okay, Alice. I get the point. Can we get on with this now?"

Alice gave a full-bodied laugh at having won a tug of war with her old friend. "Sure thing, Connie. It's pretty simple. Penicillin. She had an allergic reaction to penicillin."

Conrad scowled. "Her parents said she had no allergies!"

"No food allergies, but they did admit that when she was a child, she broke out in hives and an itchy rash when on a penicillin variant, so her doctor avoided prescribing penicillin-based drugs to her after that reaction. It's a sign of allergy, yes, but not dangerous."

"Well, I guess she didn't take it seriously either. I don't remember a prescription bottle being in her belongings at the house, though."

"That's where the mystery lies. She had about six-times the normal dose of penicillin in her system. In fact, some was still in her stomach contents, so she had taken it that evening. Unless you need something else, I'm wrapping her up and sending her home."

"No signs of struggle? Fingernails clean? No scratches?"

"Nothing. She was in pristine condition."

Conrad tapped his pen on his notepad. "What else had she eaten that night?"

"Dessert! Some kind of chocolate dessert is my best guess. Nothing else."

Conrad hummed.

"That must be why people say you should always eat dessert first." Alice huffed into the phone receiver. "It would be truly disappointing if your last meal was a meatloaf sandwich and you died before the Brownie Supreme was served."

Conrad shook his head, but couldn't hold back his smile. Alice's brazen manner made many people recoil, but he knew she made things light to find a manageable way to keep living with all the death around her. "Yes, it would be. In fact, I think you've convinced me to have a second muffin!"

"I'll send the reports over. Call me if you need anything else."

"I will. Thank you, Alice. Take care."

Conrad disconnected the call and immediately called Cora Mae. She had only asked about these lab results four or five times, but he knew she would want to know. This resolution should put Cora's mind at ease and now the community could stop gossiping about a murderer on the loose.

Joyce Miller arrived first with her knitting bag in hand, because Joyce was always early. "Hello, ladies! I was so happy to hear we are starting the group again. I miss seeing everyone."

"Come in!" Peggy led Joyce to the sofa in the back of the store. "We kept talking about starting the Tuesday Tea group up again and things just kept delaying us. Cutting a hole in our wall and then opening The Salty Shipper next door was a bigger project than I expected."

"Isn't that always the way?" Joyce walked by the

sofa and chose a straight-backed chair beside the sofa instead. Joyce was a prim petite lady with perfect posture and a pro at everything she tried, however, she had no passion for random adventure. She preferred practical patterns with purpose and was working on a filet crocheted curtain valance pattern in a bright blue Number 10 cotton for her kitchen window. After retiring from her long career at the Spicetown Library, taking care of her husband, Bert, was her main focus. "Every little project Bert starts turns into a month-long crusade. Sometimes, he never finishes the project at all, but I can't nag at him about it. If I do, he brings up all the half-finished items I have stashed away for a rainy day."

Peggy waved when she saw Dorleen hold the door open for Grace to walk through with a platter of treats in her hands. Her craft bag and purse were hanging from the crook of her arm and slapping against her leg as she walked.

Arlene rushed around the counter with her hands out. "Here, let me take that from you."

"Thank you, dear." Grace Keslar wrenched her bags from her arm and carried them to the sofa with Dorleen following. They both settled on the sofa as Arlene busied herself around the coffee table to make room for the snacks.

Grace started to pull her knitting project from her bag, the same knitting project she had worked on all last winter at their Tuesday Tea meetings, but stopped suddenly and turned her head from left to right. "Is there a dog in here?"

Peggy's eyes shifted nervously. "Does he smell bad? I just gave him a bath on Sunday."

"No, not at all. I just had a feeling...."

Peggy pointed to the dog bed just inside the storage room door. Sully was lounging comfortably, but was alert and watching all the excitement of the visitors. "That's Sully."

"Oh, yes! I remember now. We met on the street one day when you were walking him. I completely forgot you had a new pet. How nice that he gets to come to work with you. I know Chauncey would have loved it if you could have all come to the house again. He enjoyed the Tuesday Teas."

"How is Chauncey?" Joyce did not have a pet, but she had always been fascinated with Grace Keslar's cat. He had such an intelligent gaze, and he responded to Grace as if he understood every word she spoke.

"He is as busy as ever. We still have weekly guests that he must attend to and he takes his job very seriously." Grace gave a curt nod with a muffled chuckle. "I'm sure the house couldn't run without him."

"I think Sully's only talent is working as a door stop. When the weather was cool this spring, we could use his cage to prop open the back door to let some air in. His weight in the cage is what kept the door open."

Everyone looked over at Sully, and Peggy could see his little stump of a tail wagging. He knew he was being talked about and he loved the attention. Once Dorleen got tickled over something, though, it was difficult to calm her back down, and Dorleen was still shaking with laughter when Mildred walked in the door.

"Hey, everybody. Sorry I'm late, but I couldn't get a parking spot out front. Is that sassy store open already? There seems to be a lot of cars out there today." Mildred sat at the end of the couch and pulled out her knitting project, a yellow cotton baby blanket.

"Not yet. I'm not sure what the official opening date is." Arlene walked around the coffee table. "Can I get anyone a drink? Coffee or tea?"

"Just a cup of hot water for me." Joyce stashed tea bags in her purse and craft bag, so she was always prepared.

"I'd like some tea." Mildred nodded. "Whatever you have is fine."

Arlene disappeared into the back room, and Peggy took a seat. "I guess everyone heard that a young girl died last week. She worked over at the Sassafras store."

"She died right across the street from my house!" Mildred shouted. "There was all kinds of commotion going on over there."

"Oh my!" Dorleen jumped in her seat. "Yes, I heard

about it at the beauty shop. I rarely read the paper anymore, but I guess I should. I couldn't believe it. Have they found out why she died?"

"I haven't heard anything, and the girls across the street don't seem to know. I don't see them every day but I always ask if there's any news." Peggy reached for a cookie on the tray.

"I met one of them." Grace covered her mouth with her hand as her eyes shifted to the side in thought. "I can't remember her name. She was at the new clinic last week and we were both sitting in the waiting room. She was blond and a little heavyset. Nice girl. She told me she was feeling under the weather and she didn't have time to be sick because they were working on the new store." Grace chuckled. "No one wants to dedicate time for illness, but she was there for a sore throat. I made sure I didn't get too close! I was healthy when I walked in there!"

"Sounds like Heather." Arlene sat steaming mugs in front of Mildred and Joyce. "Yes, she's a sweet girl. She's been staying out there on Cumin Court in Hazel Redding's model home. Clyde didn't have any rentals available for them when they arrived, and the Nutmeg Inn was full."

"The model home?" Joyce straightened in her chair. "That's right behind my house and there isn't a young girl staying there. There's an older man in there and he's not friendly. I've waved at him a few times and he just ignores me."

"Oh, well, maybe I misunderstood Clyde." Arlene frowned. "He's been very busy lately with all these girls needing a place, two new commercial rentals to handle, and the new financial planner who is looking for a house."

"Who is the new financial planner?" Dorleen's eyes squinted as she looked around at all the ladies, afraid to ask what she really wanted to know.

Peggy glanced at Arlene and spoke first. "Ross Miniken. He's retired from up north somewhere and wants to just work part-time. He's renting Jacob Hart's old building around the corner."

"How nice," Grace said. "I'm glad they finally worked it all out. I know the owner did not want to rent at first."

"No, he wouldn't rent it. Jeremiah sold it to an investment group and Ross is renting from them instead." Peggy glanced at Grace, but she gave no indication that she knew about it.

"That little girl you met must be a friend to the one that died," Mildred leaned forward on the sofa to talk over Dorleen's knitting and speak to Grace. "I saw her visit the girl the night before she died."

Peggy's head jerked. "The night before? Do you mean last Wednesday?"

"Yep. She parked her little car in the street in front of my house and walked up to the front door with a pie in her hands. It looked like one of those tasteless ones you get at the grocery with the plastic top. It was not from Vicki's." Mildred shook her head in disapproval. If you couldn't make it yourself, you should at least buy it from the Fennel Street Bakery.

"Did she stay long?" Peggy made eye contact with Arlene and then looked at Mildred.

"Oh, no. She just gave her the pie and left right away. She wasn't there long."

Peggy tried to keep the alarm from her voice. "What time was that? Do you remember? Did you see Herman Latley, too? He said he went by that same evening."

"Oh, yeah!" Mildred dropped her project in her lap. "I talked to him a minute before he left. I saw him standing out near his truck on the street and I hollered at him. I'm needing a little work done and wanted to see if he could do it when Charlie wasn't around. Charlie never wants me to hire anything done, but he doesn't do a darn thing around the house."

Peggy smiled and waited for the other ladies to agree with Mildred's frustration before asking again. "Was that before or after Heather stopped by with the pie?"

"Oh, that was after. It was almost getting dark by

then." Mildred picked up her knitting to start a new row.

"Hello!" The door chimes jingled, and Mavis Bell pushed through the door with egg cartons stacked to her chin. "I was just passing by and thought I'd stop in and see if anyone wanted fresh eggs!"

Chapter 24

"Chief? Have you got a minute?" Eugene Tabor leaned in the doorway to Conrad's office with a notebook in his hand and Conrad waved him in. "I found a couple of things out I wanted to tell you about."

"About Ross Miniken?" Conrad removed his reading glasses and rubbed his eyes. Autopsy reports were not riveting reading.

"Yeah, but also about Regina Adkins and this Sassafras business." Eugene took the chair across the desk from Conrad and put his notepad on his knee. "Did you know there were other deaths?"

"Regina told me she'd lost an employee before." Conrad scratched his head. He hadn't paid much attention to the statement at the time. "She said it was an accident, I think. Hit and run, maybe?"

Eugene nodded. "Elizabeth Carney, 19. She was riding a bike in Georgetown, Kentucky. She was working at a Sassafras store there in Georgetown."

Conrad nodded. It was tragic, but he didn't see the connection to Brook Calvert.

"Earlier that same year, there was another death in a hotel in Lexington, Kentucky. Lori Cunningham, age 27, drowned in the hotel pool. There was head trauma, but they ruled it was accidental. She was allegedly swimming alone and they thought she injured herself diving."

"This girl also worked for Regina?"

"She did." Tabor was bouncing his foot and waiting for Conrad's reaction. "It sounds like she was supposed to be the manager at that store, but it hadn't opened yet."

"Now, that's a little too much coincidence." Conrad leaned back in his chair. "Don't you think?"

Tabor inhaled and nodded his head. "I think so. Most people go their whole life and have maybe one person they know who suffers an accidental death. Regina has had three in the last two years and they were all her employees. I think that's a clear pattern."

Conrad was trying to remember how long each of the current employees had worked for Regina. Maybe they didn't know about the history. He would need to pull those reports up again. "See if you can get copies of those Kentucky reports. Anything else?"

“I think I finally nailed down Ross Miniken. This is going to sound strange, but I think he changed his name when he got married.” Tabor’s eyebrows went up. “I mean, it looks that way. I just never knew guys did that.”

“Yeah, they do sometimes, but it’s not common. If the guy has no family and the woman does, I’ve seen it done. Who did he marry? Somebody with money?”

“It looks like his real name is Randal Ross Beecher. Beecher is certified with the State as a financial planner. He’s not a CPA and doesn’t have any advanced degrees, but he had a firm near Toledo until he retired last year. The website is still up and the picture looks like Ross Miniken.”

“Hmm, I guess that’s good to know. If he went through the court to change his name, there’s nothing illegal about that.”

Tabor made a note on his pad. “I haven’t checked the court records yet, but I’ll do that.”

“Where’s the wife?”

“She’s dead.” Tabor shrugged. “I found an obituary, but they never tell you much. It mentions her husband, Ross. It doesn’t give his last name, but that’s actually how I started down this path when I began looking for him.”

“Well, at least that mystery is solved.” Conrad still had questions about Ross that he’d like to flush out in the future, but he had no police reason to follow-up on it. He was getting as nosy as Cora Mae. "Email me the reports on the other Sassafras deaths. I'm going to check over the girl's statements. I might need to talk to them again."

"Right, Chief."

"I'm so sorry I couldn't make it earlier." Cora Mae had arrived at the knitting group just as everyone was breaking up to leave. "I didn't even bring my bag. I knew I'd be too late to join in, but my meeting ran long."

"We understand." Arlene patted Cora on the back. "At least you got to see everyone."

"Yes, that was nice." Cora Mae smiled. "I'm so glad Grace made it to the meeting. I worry about her out at the mansion all alone. I always think I'm going to get out there to visit, but...." Cora waved her hands helplessly. She had so many plans and so little time.

"Have a seat!" Peggy pointed to the sofa. "You can at least have one of Imogene's treats. They're delicious."

"I wish I could, but Eleanor Cline is coming by at 3:30 to work out the details for the next play. Did I tell you about that already?"

"Yes, the Christmas play that doesn't sound like a Christmas play," Peggy chuckled. "I distinctly remember no wardrobe changes were needed. That was my favorite part!"

"That's correct. The whole play happens in one place, so we don't have a bunch of sets to create either. I thought we needed an easy one for a change." Cora's shrug of relief caused her bangs to flutter, and she fluffed her hair back into place. "I just hope Eleanor doesn't make it complicated."

Peggy raised an eyebrow in doubt. Eleanor loved a challenge, but she never realized that for everyone else, *she* was the challenge. "I'm not complaining."

"Well, the casting call should be in the newspaper by next week. That's what we're finalizing today." Cora turned toward Peggy and lowered her voice, although there were no customers in the store. "The other thing I wanted to mention to you, is they found a cause of death for the little girl across the street."

Arlene gasped. "What was it?"

"An allergic reaction." Cora nodded curtly. "The poor child was allergic to penicillin. Can you believe it?"

"That's so sad." Arlene's hand patted her own chest as her brow creased. "I feel so terrible for her family. They must be devastated."

"They must." Cora Mae turned toward the door.

"Have you been in Sassafras yet?" Peggy pointed across the street.

"Just for a minute. I went to pay my respects. Do

you know when they plan to open?" Cora looked out the window. "It looks like the Chief is paying them a visit. He's walking down that way now."

Arlene stepped over to the window to see. "He's been there several times. Maybe he's there to tell them about the cause of death. Did he just find out today?"

"Yes, the coroner called him this morning. Her parents were still here in town the last I heard. I assume they will be returning home now. I wondered if the girls were going to close up for a while so they could attend services for her."

"I doubt that." Peggy huffed and tossed the embroidery kits back on the display table. "They don't seem to care at all. I've been over there several times and it is business as usual. Not just Regina. It's all of them!"

Cora Mae frowned. "That is odd." Cora slipped her phone from her front pocket and glanced at the screen. "Well, Amanda needs me, so I better get going."

Arlene chuckled and held the door open for Cora Mae as they said their goodbyes, both risking furtive glances across the street to look for activity. Peggy just stared off into her own deep thoughts.

Arlene sighed once the door closed behind Cora Mae. "Wasn't that a nice group meeting? I missed all of those Tuesday Teas you had at Grace's mansion, so it's been over a year since I was able to take part. I'm so glad it's back at the shop now."

Peggy ignored Arlene's swoon. "I need to talk to Chief Harris. There are things I need to make sure he knows. Maybe he does already know them, but I don't know if he knows them, and if he doesn't know them, I couldn't live with myself if I didn't tell him."

"What? What things?" Arlene's forehead wrinkled in alarm.

"All of these pieces are fitting together now. All of this is really something.... I think, but maybe I'm wrong."

Arlene walked closer and spoke louder. "What pieces? What things?"

"Little things I've seen and heard, they all seemed unimportant at first. Now, it is starting to make sense to me and it's not good! I even think I know who did it."

"Who did what? What are we talking about?" Arlene scowled at being left behind in something that was obviously dramatic and significant.

Peggy grabbed Arlene's hands. "I don't think Brook's death was an accident."

Speechless, they both turned and looked out the front window.

Chapter 25

"Hey, Chief." Asher called out as Conrad walked in the door. "You missed Clyde Newman's return call, but he said he'd call back as soon as he's done with his next appointment."

Conrad nodded and muttered a thank you Roy could not possibly hear.

"Learn anything new down there?" Eugene Tabor stood up from behind his desk and adjusted his belt.

"Not a thing, but they've all been told now. They didn't have much to say. I tried to get Regina aside to ask about the other deaths, but she was in the middle of arguing with the internet company about being late for her installation appointment, so I'll try talking to her again in the morning."

"I'm headed back out. Is there anything you need

me to do?"

"Has Georgia been back in? She went out to Mavis Bell's place to get some prints and I haven't heard back from her. You might check and see if she needs help."

"Will do, Chief."

Conrad stomped down the hallway toward his office, seeking a moment of peace. He needed to sort out all these little nuances and decide if he was going to accept everything on face value just as the parents, coworkers, and the mayor had done. No one seemed to expect anything more from him, but he didn't feel like the situation was properly resolved. Maybe he was just asking for trouble.

"Afternoon, Peggy. What can I do for you?" Roy Asher beamed a winning smile and had to admit that he was beginning to appreciate working in dispatch. Greeting people that were seeking out help instead of chasing people that wanted to get away from him was a refreshing change.

"I'd like to speak to the chief for just a minute. It shouldn't take long. I tried to catch him when he was downtown, but I had a customer in the store and couldn't talk. Do you think he'd see me?"

"Aw, let me check. If he's not on the phone, I'm sure he'd be okay with that." Roy tapped the button for Conrad's office intercom, and Peggy stepped back near the visitors' chairs to wait. Before she could sit, Roy waved her forward. "You can go on back to his office."

"Thanks, Roy!" Peggy walked down the hallway hesitantly. She knew this whole affair was none of her business, and she didn't want to make him angry, but she had to get it all out.

"Hi, Chief. Thanks for seeing me." Peggy waited in the doorway timidly, bracing herself for his reaction.

"Hi, Peggy. Have a seat. How can I help you?"

Peggy sat on the edge of the visitor chair and began with the first item on her talking points list. She had rehearsed this on her way to the station. "I heard that Brook died from an allergic reaction. This may sound like a strange question, but I was wondering if you ever located her mobile phone."

"Hmm, I don't recall. I wasn't the one who collected her belongings, but I can look through the report." Conrad turned to his computer monitor where he had Brook's case record already opened on his screen. "Is there some reason you're asking?"

"Well, I saw an extra phone at Sassafras a couple of days ago and I thought it might be hers. It was pink and had rhinestones on the case." Peggy waited for Conrad to read the report, but had to fill the silence. "I could be wrong. I had forgotten all about it, too, but when I saw a pink phone today, when Cora Mae pulled out her phone and it had a pink case, it reminded me that I did see that extra phone in someone's purse. I think it was Heather's purse, but all of those girls are always on their phone or carrying it around with them, and this one was just lying there in her open purse. I thought you might need to know about it if you were looking for it."

"Thank you for the tip. I don't know if anyone is looking, but I'm sure her parents would like it back."

"I was just thinking if I was having an allergic reaction to something, I'd be trying to call 9-1-1 for help, but maybe she couldn't. Maybe she didn't have her phone."

Conrad didn't see any mention of a phone in the report inventory, and he was disappointed in himself for not noticing that absence.

"Uh, another thing, you know the girls that work there were all staying in different houses around town because the Nutmeg Inn was full."

"Yes," Conrad said as he folded his hands in front of him on the desk.

"Well, Heather was supposed to be staying in Hazel Redding's old house, the model home on Cumin Court, but Joyce Miller said there is an older man in there. She's never seen a young girl there." Peggy paused, but Conrad did not react. "I don't know if that matters, but I wanted you to know."

Conrad would check with Clyde Newman on that when they finally connected. Perhaps he should call the

Nutmeg Inn, too. Levi Nauchtman could tell him if there had been a change in reservations. There could be a simple explanation for all that. "Okay, but I'm sure those housing arrangements were subject to change, since it was temporary housing. Red Pepper Realty is handling all of that."

"Yes, I know. I just wanted you to know that there was a change." Peggy looked down at her own clasped hands in her lap. All of these pieces she thought were so significant were now sounding trivial when she tried to explain them.

"I'll look into it."

"Uh, and the penicillin. Do you know where that came from? Did Brook have a prescription for penicillin or have some in her purse when you found her?"

Conrad frowned. He hadn't gotten that far yet, but he was sure he would have remembered that. "And why do you ask that?"

"I'm not trying to be nosy. Really, I'm not. I just hear things and see things. You know how this town is, and then I get worried no one has told you or that what I know might make a difference somehow. I know you don't want to hear my crazy thoughts, but I just didn't want to ignore these things that need to be said, and I'm really sorry to be wasting your time like this."

Conrad smiled. "You're talking at Harvey Salzman speed now. Let's slow it down and have a moment of

Zen."

"Oh, sorry." Peggy felt embarrassment flood her face with heat even though she knew he was teasing her. He was right. She needed to relax and do what she came for. "I wondered because I heard Heather was at the clinic last week for a sore throat and she may have been prescribed penicillin."

"Okay." Conrad nodded. Nothing nefarious necessarily, but noteworthy. People shared prescriptions all the time when they shouldn't, but Alice had said the dose was really high.

"Just one more question, and then I'll leave you alone. I promise."

Conrad smiled patiently. "You are not bothering me at all. I appreciate your observations. I'm just not in a position to answer your questions or give out information to the public. I hope you understand that." It had to be a one-way street, and most informants were not satisfied with that arrangement.

"I understand. I don't mean to question you. It just comes out of my head that way." Peggy held her hands up and paused. She couldn't think of any other way to do it. She had to ask the question. "Did you test the pie?"

"The pie?" Conrad frowned. Peggy had stumped him with that one. "What pie?"

"Well, assuming that Heather was prescribed penicillin for her throat last week and Brook was not sick,

I thought maybe the penicillin was in the cream pie that Heather took to Brook the night she died."

After sitting in silence for an eternity of fifteen seconds, Peggy elaborated. "Mildred Mays lives across the street from the house that Brook was staying in. I assume you know that Herman Latley was over there that night to fix the air conditioning. I mean, Saucy knows about that, so I'm sure you do, too. And if you interviewed Herman, he probably told you she was fine that evening and she sat there eating pie at the kitchen counter while he fixed the thermostat. Am I right? Oh, sorry, another question." Peggy waved her hand to erase the comment and moved on.

"Anyway, before Herman arrived Mildred saw a young blond girl bring a store-bought pie to Brook. She rang the bell, gave the pie to her, and left. Now, they had just had a big celebratory luncheon that day and there was a chocolate pie involved. I know, because they stored some items in my refrigerator the day of the party and the night after, but the pie was only there in the morning. It didn't come back after lunch, so I thought the girls had finished it. Now, I think maybe it was left behind at the store and Heather took it to Brook because she purchased it or maybe because she especially liked it. I don't know.

"That leads me to a question, but I'm not asking. I'm just talking out loud. Could Heather have known

Brook had an allergy to penicillin? Could she have opened the penicillin capsules and sprinkled it over the meringue before taking the pie to Brook? If there was a lot of pie left over, maybe it's still in the refrigerator at the rental house and you could test it."

Peggy sat back in her chair and stared at Conrad. She was out of questions and he was looking down at his desktop. The silence was awkward and she was ready to leave, but she felt better for having said it all. "That's all I have, I think. I just wanted to get it off my chest. I don't expect any answers."

Peggy stood up and turned toward the door just as a memory came out of nowhere and almost knocked her back. "Oh, one more little thing. I forgot all about this. I heard from one girl that this is not the first employee's death that's happened. Maybe that doesn't make a pattern, but it is an eerie coincidence. Don't you think?" Peggy jerked and erased her question again from the imaginary chalkboard. "It's entirely hearsay, and I don't have any details, but Regina should be able to tell you, unless she has already. Okay? Okay. I'll get out of your hair now. Thanks for seeing me."

Conrad nodded, but before he could speak, Peggy rushed out the door and down the hall.

Once back in the lobby, she relaxed from the relief that Conrad had not scolded her for meddling, and she waved goodbye to Roy, who was chatting on the phone.

Whew, so glad that is over!

Chapter 26

After staring into space to process the picture Peggy had painted, Conrad rapidly scribbled all of his questions on a piece of paper. He rarely used the lists he made, but the act of writing each item etched them into his memory and once there, he could rearrange them as needed. Peggy had just voiced all the concerns he had been feeling and validated that he was not making something out of nothing.

Glancing at the clock, he jumped up from his desk and headed to dispatch. He only had an hour before shift change, and he needed to talk to Georgia and Eugene. "Asher, I need a twenty on Tabor and Marks."

Roy jumped in his seat and held his shoulders back. Conrad's serious tone always set him on edge, even when he was not the target. "They're both at Mavis Bell's home finishing up. Georgia's doing a footprint plaster. Do you need them called back in?"

"No, I'm headed out that way. If Clyde Newman calls, let me know. I'd still like to talk to him if I'm free when he calls back."

"Gotcha, Chief." Roy spun his chair around and scooted over to one side when he heard Conrad snap his fingers. Briscoe shot out from under the counter and stood still for his lead to be attached before following Conrad down the hallway and out the side door.

Although Briscoe's skills weren't needed, Conrad felt guilty if he didn't give him a little action each day. Briscoe was showing signs of aging, so Dr. Morgan had put him on a joint supplement, but his nose still worked fine and he wanted to be involved in Conrad's day.

Driving down North Road, he could see the model home on Cumin Court that Heather had been given as a rental. It had never been listed for sale after Hazel Redding left Spicetown. The scandal she caused, almost forgotten now, had spurred the creation of two new subdivisions. The annexation had moved the city limits of Spicetown a few miles north and increased his workload during development, but it had been quiet now for a while. Seeing a dark sedan in the driveway, he slowed. He knew it was not Heather's car, but the out-of-state license plate caught his eye and he pulled in behind the car, asking Roy to run the tag number.

Before Roy could provide the information, he recognized the man strolling out the front door and toward his car. Conrad lowered his car window and turned down his radio.

"Evening, Chief. Is there something I can help you with?" Mr. Abbott, the difficult railroad fanatic, walked up to the window and eyed the large dog peering over Conrad's shoulder.

"Hello, Mr. Abbott. I just stopped by when I saw the car because I was looking for someone. Are you renting the house?"

"You must be looking for Heather." Mr. Abbott nodded. "I gave her my room at the Nutmeg Inn and took the house. She was a little spooked being out here alone, and it was easier for her to be close to work. It's all on the up and up, I assure you."

"Oh, I'm sure it is. She just hadn't mentioned it to me and I didn't realize you even knew each other."

"Yes, she's my step-daughter." Mr. Abbott smiled. "We didn't travel here together, but my wife, her mother, asked me to keep an eye on her. It would probably be best if you didn't share that last part with her."

Conrad chuckled. "That's quite a coincidence that you both ended up here at the same time." Even Heather should have been able to figure that out.

Mr. Abbott nodded and stepped further from the car when Briscoe's nose popped out the window with flared nostrils. “Well, I’m not staying as long. I plan to leave tomorrow morning, but if I see Heather, I’ll let her know you are looking for her.”

“Oh, that’s not necessary. I’ll find her at the store. Safe travels.” Conrad patted Briscoe’s cheek before raising his window as he backed out of the driveway.

Mavis Bell’s land was due north, just past the two subdivisions. Her new greenhouse and farmland were directly adjacent to the back yards of the homes on Lavender Lane, but her home was across the road to his left. Two squad cars were parked in the drive when Conrad pulled up.

Hooking Briscoe to his leash, they both stretched their legs before approaching the back of the house. “How many cops does it take to capture a footprint?”

Eugene Tabor laughed when he saw Conrad’s smile. “The right answer must be three!”

Georgia’s brow furrowed. Still on her knees in the mulch around Mavis’ bushes, she hadn’t seen Conrad’s smile. “Sorry, Chief. I just wanted to make sure this was right. I haven’t done a plaster kit in a decade.”

Police equipment and techniques changed just like technology, and Georgia’s statement reaffirmed that his dispatch rotation plan was beneficial. “Aw, I’m just teasing. Take your time. I was just out this way, and thought I’d drop by. I wanted to ask you both a couple of questions about the Brook Calvert case.”

Eugene stepped back into the grass. "Asher told us it was a penicillin allergy."

"Yeah, but I had a couple of questions after I read the report."

Georgia rocked back to her feet. The plaster was still drying. "Did I miss something?"

"Maybe not." Conrad held up his hand to quell Georgia's lack of confidence. "I just wondered about Brook's phone. I didn't see it in the evidence list you compiled and it seems a little odd for a young person not to have one. It's usually in their hand at all times."

Eugene's eyes squinted in concern. "You're right, Chief, but I didn't find one. Maybe we need to search her car again. It could be between the seats and we missed it."

"Good idea!" Conrad pointed at Eugene and knew he would follow up. "The other question was the refrigerator. I know you collected the trash, but there wasn't any mention of food containers, except for a drink can."

"I'm sure she had to eat out every day, Chief," Georgia said. "The place doesn't have dishes or cooking utensils."

"All the more reason for food containers!" Eugene threw his hands out to his sides. "You would think she would have a sandwich wrapper or pizza box in the trash."

"Yes, but also because I talked to Herman Latley, who was there the evening she died. I don't know if you read that report, but he said she was sitting at the bar in the kitchen eating pie while he worked."

Eugene nodded. "Yeah, he said she was friendly and seemed fine."

"If the pie container wasn't in the trash, did we check the fridge?" Conrad's eyebrows rose in question, trying to soften any accusation. "She couldn't eat pie from her hand."

"I didn't." Georgia looked guiltily at Eugene, who also shook his head. "I'm sorry, Chief. I missed it. I should have, but I was just thinking the place was empty and I just.... I screwed up."

"I got a call in to Clyde already about another issue, so I'll just ask him if he'll let us back in the house. I don't think he would have the place cleaned without checking with me first. If there's something in there, it'll still be there, but if we find something, we need to get it to Paxton right away, because it needs to be tested."

"You think there is penicillin in the pie?" Georgia's face was etched with concern as she realized there might be more to this story.

"There might be. There's a witness that saw a young woman bring that pie to her house before Herman got there. I'm not sure yet, but it might have been Heather Halstrom. That's who I'm looking for now. She was supposed to be staying in the old Redding model home, but her step-father, Mr. Abbott, is there and he says he gave Heather his room at the Nutmeg Inn. Did she mention to either of you she was staying at the inn?"

"No," Georgia shook her head. "I asked her for contact information and she gave me her phone number. She said she was at the store all the time, if we needed her. I didn't ask where she was staying." Georgia shook her head again and scowled at her own shortcomings.

"I interviewed her and I didn't ask either. We all overlook things, especially when we think it's accidental. That's why I always say to work it like it's real. You just never know when something little becomes something big. I should listen to my own advice!" Conrad shrugged. "Nobody is perfect. That's why working alone is a mistake. It takes a collection of minds to cover everything."

"You know, Chief," Georgia held up her finger. "That Mr. Abbott you mentioned is the guy that Mavis thinks is behind all of this. She thinks he might have been trying to break into her house. I didn't know that he was Heather's step-father."

"Yeah, he seems to want Mavis to sell a family heirloom and she's not interested. She might be right."

"Do you think so?" Georgia frowned down at the plaster cast she had spent far too long creating.

"It looks like a small shoe size, and Mr. Abbott is a

little guy. He's only about five foot six and wears dress shoes that wouldn't have tread on the bottom. I'm not sure he's fit enough to hoist himself up through a window that's four feet from ground level, though. That might be a struggle for him."

"I'm sure Mavis wasn't thinking about the physical requirement." Georgia looked up at the window, speculating whether she could get herself up there.

"It doesn't mean he didn't pay someone to do it." Eugene stroked Briscoe's head.

"That's true. Mavis mentioned that to me and I think we need to dig a little deeper into him, too." Conrad pointed at Eugene. "Tabor, when you get back to the office, see if you can find out some background on this guy. His first name is Harold."

"Will do, Chief." Tabor nodded. "I think we're done here."

Conrad tugged gently on Briscoe's leash. "I'm going back to town to find Heather."

Chapter 27

Peggy returned to the craft store and was relieved it was without customers. She had stopped in the drugstore on the corner and bought two ice cream sandwiches on her walk back and she had been forced to walk fast to keep them from melting. Holding one out for Arlene, she ripped the paper off the top of her own sandwich and took a bite. "Eat quick! They were melting fast out there."

Arlene followed her lead and took a big bite. "I'm so glad you remembered! I've been craving this all afternoon, even though I shouldn't eat it."

"Nah, it's an excellent source of calcium. Nothing to feel guilty about."

Arlene smiled. "I see your head is still attached, so I guess the chief didn't take it off."

Peggy slurped around the edges of the melting ice

cream and laughed. “No, he was patient with me.” Peggy grabbed a handful of napkins as they worked quickly to finish. “Did I miss anything around here while I was gone?”

“A few things. Regina’s flower order arrived and the package pickup guy came by.” Arlene finished her ice cream and tossed the wrapper into the trash. “Let me wash my hands first.”

Peggy scooped some ice cream out of the center of her sandwich and let Sully lick it from her finger while Arlene was out of sight, before following her back to the storeroom to wash up once she finished off the rest.

Drying her hands, Arlene stepped back so Peggy could rinse her hands. “Cora Mae called while you were out. She was looking for her reading glasses and thought she might have left them here. She said the ad may be in the paper as early as tomorrow for play auditions. Eleanor is in a hurry to get started. She was getting ready to run it over to the paper office when she called.”

“Saucy said there were only five or six actors for this play, so it should be an easy one.”

“I told her you talked to Jason earlier and asked if she was going to let the bank buy the Thanksgiving turkeys, and she said she was going to talk to them. She sounded excited about it.”

“That’s good. I’m sure that will relieve some of her worries.”

Arlene cleared her throat. "You also missed Eleanor Cline."

Peggy hummed while she debated whether to show gratitude or remain silent. As director of the community plays and Cinnamon High School's drama teacher, Eleanor had been known to overstep the boundaries of her authority on more than one occasion.

Arlene handed Peggy the towel. "I know. You're feeling lucky, but she actually brought us some paying business this time, not just criticism."

"That's a pleasant change!"

Arlene nodded. "She brought in some fabric and a pattern. It's the black velvet over there on the back table."

Walking out of the storage room, Peggy detoured to the back and fingered the fabric. "I wonder where she bought it."

"I told her we would have ordered it for her if we'd known she wanted it, but she said she prefers to see things first." Arlene sniffed and rolled her eyes to mimic Eleanor's response.

Peggy chuckled. Arlene didn't know how great her talents at mockery were. She should be acting in these community plays. "Did she give you measurements?"

"I took them while she was here. I had to move Sully's cage to the back room and put him in it before she would agree to give me five minutes to do that, but I got them. I knew we didn't want to make her come back in more than was absolutely necessary."

Peggy nodded as she glanced down at her lounging English bulldog. "She doesn't like Sully?"

"Oh, no! She was appalled that we would have an animal in a retail store. She was certain we were losing business because of it. I told her that her complaint was our very first and she explained to me that some people are allergic to pet dander."

"Oh, really? Is Eleanor allergic to pet dander?" Peggy cocked her head and smiled, anticipating the answer.

"Of course not. She's just an animal hater." Arlene sneered.

Peggy laughed and scratched at Sully's ear. "Sully, you are going to every play practice with me from now on!"

"He makes an excellent Eleanor repellent." Arlene smiled. "So, what did the Chief say?"

"Not much. I mean, he can't give me information, but at least he listened to what I had to say without making me feel like a fool for saying it. I got the feeling, though, that I wasn't really telling him anything he didn't already know."

"So, he knows Brook's death wasn't an accident."

Peggy winced. "Well, nobody really knows that yet, but he didn't ridicule my suggestion that it might not be, so I think he knows."

"Good! That means he isn't throwing in the towel. If someone did this to that young girl, they should have to pay for it!" Arlene pounded her fist on the counter. "I was thinking after you left, it could be Eden. You know, Mildred said a blond girl. Eden is a young blond girl, too, and she did not like Brook at all."

Peggy hadn't thought about that, but Mildred had said heavyset. Eden was a small girl. She never had much to say, but she gave off a negative vibe all the time. "You're right. I told the chief that it was Mildred that saw her, so maybe he'll go talk to her and get a better description. Eden could have taken the penicillin from Heather's purse and stashed the phone in there. Her purse doesn't close. It's one of those loose bags that is always open at the top and she leaves it sitting in a chair all day exposed. It sounds rather devious, but murderers usually are!"

Arlene shook her head slowly and made a clicking noise with her tongue. "It's always the quiet ones."

Conrad backed out of the Nutmeg Inn parking lot to drive around the block to Sassafras. Seeing Heather's car at the inn, he had stopped there first, but Gretchen told him that Heather had walked to the store that morning and hadn't yet returned. After talking to Mildred Mays on the phone while he drove back to town, he knew he needed to find Heather today.

Glancing through the plate glass doors, he saw a flurry of activity in every corner. Missy was hanging clothing on racks, and Eden was behind a counter, unwrapping smaller items secured in tissue paper. Kim had a rolling cart of stacked boxes and Heather was using a utility knife to cut the boxes open. When he strolled into Sassafras with Briscoe on a leash, the room fell silent.

Conrad smiled. "Good afternoon, ladies. Is Regina around anywhere?"

"Yeah, she's upstairs. I'll get her, Chief." Heather placed the knife on the counter and ran up the steps.

"Beautiful dog, Chief." Kim tipped the handcart back flat on the floor. "What's his name?"

"This is Officer Briscoe." Briscoe's head pivoted up to look at Conrad. "He's a police dog."

"Oh, I see." Kim nodded. "No petting or anything, right? He's working."

"That's right. Have you settled on an opening date for the store yet?" Conrad looked around and thought it looked close to being done.

"No, we're a little off schedule right now." Kim

smiled as Regina walked down the stairs with Heather behind her.

"Are you eager to start shopping, Chief?" Regina said sarcastically.

"No, I'm just preparing for the next traffic jam."

Regina nodded, accepting his sarcasm in return. "What can I do for you?"

"Well, I need a little of your time again." Looking around Regina, he nodded his head toward Heather. "And another few minutes from Heather."

"Now? Why?"

"We have a few more questions. A few loose ends to tie up. If you don't mind, I'd like to take Heather back to the station with me now and I'd appreciate it if you could run up there once you finish up here today."

"Chief, we are way behind schedule already. Can't this wait?" Regina's lack of cooperation seemed focused on her own convenience and not an anxious avoidance of meeting with the police.

Heather's lack of eye contact and attempt to blend with the background told Conrad he needed to talk to her now. She might disappear tomorrow along with her step-dad if he didn't. "Death of an employee can do that." Conrad pointed at Heather. "I'll give you a ride and someone will take you back to the inn when we are done."

Heather nodded and glanced at Regina with a silent

request for help, but Regina did not acknowledge her.

"I'll see you in an hour or so?" Conrad nodded in response to his own question and turned to follow Heather out the door.

Chapter 28

Conrad placed Heather in an interview room and left with the promise of a quick return. Briscoe settled into his dispatch dog bed as Conrad got some fresh water for his bowl.

"Chief, Clyde Newman called back, but I couldn't reach you in the car. He said he's done for the day, so you can call back anytime."

Conrad glanced at the clock on the wall and grimaced. Shift change was going to complicate this. "Let me call him real quick." Pulling out his cell phone, he dialed Clyde's number just as Eugene Tabor walked in the door.

"Clyde? It's Chief Harris."

"Hey, Chief. Sorry I kept missing you."

"Yeah, it's okay. I just need two things real quick. Have you had the house cleaned yet? If not, we really need to get back in there for just a minute. Can you meet an officer there right now?" Conrad pointed at Tabor.

"Uh, uh, yeah, sure." Clearly flustered, Clyde tried to organize his thoughts. "Nobody's touched nothin'. I promise. I can go right now."

"Good. Thank you. The second thing is just a question. You rented that Redding house out to one of those Sassafras girls, Heather Halstrom. Right?"

"Yeah, I think that's the name."

"Did you know she's not staying there? Do you know a man named Harold Abbott is staying there now? He claims they switched. He gave Heather his room at the Nutmeg Inn and she gave him the house."

"What? No!" Clyde huffed. "She can't do that. Who's this Abbott guy?"

"That's all I needed. Can you be at the other house in five minutes? I'll have an officer there waiting." Clyde lived on Bay Leaf Boulevard, but he wasn't as spry as he once was.

"Yeah, sure. I'm leaving now! Be there in a flash."

Conrad hung up the phone without a goodbye and pointed at Tabor again. "I know you've just got a few minutes left, but run over to the house and check for the pie real quick. If it's there, bring it by here and I'll get someone else to run it to Paxton."

Eugene turned and jogged out the door without a reply.

Conrad looked at Roy Asher, whose eyes were wide with confusion. "Roy, Regina Adkins will be showing up here in an hour or so. Make sure you let Sammy know to put her in an interview room and get a message to me that she's here."

"Got it, Chief." Roy grabbed a notepad and furiously scribbled a note. "What about this pie?"

"Oh!" Conrad spun around on his heel. "Don't eat it! I need Jenkins to run it over to Paxton for testing. It needs an evidence tag and an order for toxicology. Can you do that before you clock out?"

"Sure thing, Chief."

Conrad watched Roy search his desk nervously for guidance. It was something he should know how to do, but urgency could rattle Roy sometimes. "If you need help, you can get the details from Tabor when he comes back."

Hoping for the best, Conrad walked into the interview room and pulled the chair out across the table from Heather Halstrom.

Kim heard the other girls whispering near the checkout counter and saw Regina pretending not to notice. Wondering if she had been left out of something, she slid the boxes off the handcart and walked over to where Regina was flipping through messages on her phone. Speaking quietly so the others didn't hear, she interrupted Regina's social scrolling. "Is there something else going on here that I don't know about?"

"What do you mean?" Regina glanced at Kim and then disregarded her by returning to her phone display.

Perhaps Regina was hoping she would drop the issue, but overplaying her innocence had only lessened her credibility. "I know I'm new here, but I've heard the others talking about a girl in the past that died while working a store setup just like this. I know Brook is not the first and now the police are back."

"You heard what he said. It was an allergy." Regina did not look up, but slipped her phone into her back pocket and turned to open a box near her feet.

"Yeah, I heard what he said, and now he needs to interview you and Heather again. That seems a little odd to me."

Regina shook her head dismissively. "It's not an interview. I'm sure he just needs to brief me to wrap things up. I was her employer. There might be something I can do to help her parents."

Kim recoiled in confusion and took a step back. "How could you help her parents? She was not your ward. Brook was an adult, and frankly, you are not legally entitled to information about her."

Regina's jaw clenched. "When did you go to law school?"

"I didn't," Kim said calmly. Reminding herself she was speaking to her employer, she reined in the resentment from the patronizing remark. "My brother-in-law is a cop, and I know they are very particular about giving out information on any victim, dead or alive."

"Well, I guess I'll find out when I talk to him. I don't know what else he could ask me. I wasn't even there when she was found, and when I went over there that morning, they wouldn't let me in the house."

Kim looked off into the distance for a moment. "Maybe they have questions about us."

"He's already talked to all of you. You weren't there either."

"I know." Kim looked down and stared at Regina. "But maybe he thinks one of us had something to do with it."

"What? That's nonsense. It was an allergic reaction! We didn't even know she was allergic to penicillin. In fact, I'm not sure she even knew. How could any of us be involved in that?"

Kim squatted down beside Regina and opened another box. "I don't know, but something doesn't feel right." Lowering her voice, Kim gestured toward Missy and Eden, who were talking near the entrance to the back room. "All the whispers and private chats speculating about conspiracy theories has me on edge, like there is some dark secret here that I don't know." Kim turned toward Regina. "What happened to the other girl?"

Regina rocked back to sit on the floor and folded her legs in front of her. "I assume they're talking about Lori. She died from a diving accident in the hotel pool."

Kim felt a knot in her throat. "How awful. Were you all there when it happened?"

"No, none of us. She wanted to go for a swim after we came back from dinner one evening, but no one else wanted to go. We all just went to our room. She loved the water. She had been on the swim team in high school and never missed a chance to swim if she could. It's the reason I picked the hotel I did." Regina smiled as her vacant gaze drifted around the room.

"She had been on a few store setups with me, and that location was going to be her store." Regina dropped her head.

"She was the lead," Kim murmured. "Just like Brook."

Regina's head popped up and her eyes locked with Kim's. "There was another before Lori."

"What?" Kim's eyebrows rose in shock.

"Beth. I didn't think of her because she actually lived in the town where we were setting up the store. She'd only been on one setup trip with me, but she'd done such a good job, that I was going to give the manager's position to her, because it was in her hometown."

"Another lead. How did she die?"

"She was hit by a car when she was riding her bike home from the store. It was a hit and run, so they never found out who did it, as far as I know."

"This is a little eerie. Don't you think?" Kim's shock had settled into a heightened awareness that she might be in the presence of a murderer.

"It is tragic. They were all so young. I know I seem unfeeling, but this is just not the first tragedy I've been through." Regina was too self-absorbed to make the connection.

"I think I need some fresh air. I'm going to walk over and get a snack. Can I get you anything?" Kim stood up, but didn't look at the other girls. She didn't want to extend the offer, but she also didn't want to be killed for overlooking them.

"No, I'm fine, but hey, could you run across the street and pick up our flowers? Peggy texted me they arrived today. We can start setting up the display cases with them in the morning."

"I'll do that." Kim rushed out the door before the other girls could inquire and headed across the street. She didn't need a snack. She needed to talk to someone with an open mind.

Chapter 29

"Heather, we have a minor discrepancy in the activities Wednesday, the day before you found Brook. I'd like to go over that day again with you, if you don't mind."

"Okay." Heather sat away from the table's edge with her hands in her lap and a guarded look in her eyes.

"I want to start off by reading you your rights, so you know where you stand. You have the right to remain silent. Anything you say can and will be used against you in a court of law. You have the right to an attorney. If you cannot afford an attorney, one will be appointed for you. Okay?"

"Wait!" Heather scowled just as a quiet tap was heard on the interview room door.

"I'll just be a second." Conrad got up and stepped outside the room.

“Sorry, Chief,” Roy whispered. “I just got the reports on those other cases that Tabor ordered. He said you wanted to see them when they came in. I didn’t know if it was urgent or not.”

“That’s good, Roy. Thanks.” Conrad scanned them quickly for names. He was curious who Regina’s employees had been during that time and if they had given statements. He expected these reports might read just like his initial reports did for Brook, before the pattern began to appear.

Slipping back inside, Conrad returned to his chair. “Sorry about that. It gets a little crazy around here at shift change. Now, what I need to review is the events of Wednesday. I know that’s been a few days ago, but I’m missing some detail, so I’m hoping you can remember what happened. That morning, Wednesday morning, everybody showed up at work with snacks for the luncheon. Is that correct? Let’s start with when you walked into work. Who was already there?”

“I don’t remember.” Heather scowled and shook her head. “I wasn’t the first one there, but I don’t think I was the last. I didn’t really pay attention.”

“What did you bring in for the luncheon?” Conrad crossed his ankle up on his other knee and put his notepad on his leg to write.

“Chips and dip. I’ve told you this already.”

“What else was offered at the luncheon and who

provided those items?" Conrad began writing what he knew already. He was certain Heather knew it, too.

"I didn't pay any attention. I just ate what was on the table." Heather huffed indignantly. "What has this got to do with anything? Am I being arrested for only bringing chips and dip? This is crazy! Do I need to call an attorney because some girl I barely knew died of an allergic reaction? What is going on here? I don't think I want to answer any more of your questions."

"I just told you what your rights are. Did you understand what I said?" Conrad leaned forward and glared at Heather.

"I'm leaving!" Heather stood up and Conrad jumped to his feet to block her from moving around the table toward the door.

"That is not your right. You are being detained for questioning. Do we need to go over your rights again?" Conrad tilted his head and feigned concern for her in hopes she had enough intelligence to be insulted. Angry interviews were usually more revealing.

Heather dropped back in her chair. "No, I just don't see where this is getting us anywhere. I've already answered these questions. I don't have any new information to give you, and what difference could any of that make now?"

"Let's jump ahead to some new information, then. Where did you go when you got off work Wednesday evening?"

"I guess I got something to eat. I don't remember. It's all the same around here. There's nothing to do and I either go to the sandwich place or the Italian place and get carry-out."

"On Tuesday night, you went out with all of your co-workers and Ross Miniken to the Ole Thyme Italian Restaurant. Does that help you remember?"

"No." Heather huffed. "That was a onetime thing."

"Ordinarily you eat alone in your room at the Nutmeg Inn?" Conrad raised an eyebrow in question and watched for her reaction. She seemed to want her temporary residence to be a secret.

"Yeah." Heather shrugged to indicate that answer was as good as any, but didn't meet Conrad's eyes.

"Today you walked to work from the inn, but you usually drive. Is it correct to assume that you drove to work on Wednesday?" Gretchen Nauchtman from the Nutmeg Inn had commented on this and thought it odd herself. Heather didn't seem the athletic type.

Heather nodded without speaking and looked down at the tabletop.

"So, Wednesday evening you left work in your car, where did you go?"

"I don't remember. Probably to the sandwich place since we went out the night before."

"Heather," Conrad said softly and waited for her

eyes to meet his. “I’m going to give you one more chance at this, and I need you to be honest with me and with yourself. I already know the answer. Where did you go between 5:30 and 6:30 Wednesday night?”

Heather turned her head to the side and didn’t speak for several seconds. “I’m not answering any more questions. I have that right.”

“You do.” Conrad nodded. “And I have the right to detain you for 72 hours.” Conrad stood up and motioned to Heather to come around the table toward him. “After you are booked, you may make a phone call. Let’s go.”

“These are really pretty! I like them much better than the ones we have at the main store. The colors are brighter.” Kim fondled the string of purple-petaled flowers.

“They aren’t exactly the same, but it’s as close as I could get to the petunias listed on the order she gave me.” Regina hadn’t seemed like much of a gardener and Peggy had hoped she wouldn’t notice the difference.

“Bellflowers.” Kim read the tag on the package and huffed. “I didn’t know what kind of flower she used, but these look more like the flower she has on the logo.”

"Yes, I wondered about that." Arlene walked around the counter. "Sassafras doesn't have a purple flower. It has a small yellow flower. I wondered why she used purple flowers in her logo."

Kim laughed. "I'm sure Regina wouldn't know a sassafras tree if it fell on her."

"It's actually a fairly common tree around here and they're lovely. Sassafras has medicinal purposes, too. My neighbor has one in her yard." Arlene smirked. "It is a spice and we are in Spicetown. She should probably expect that others will be asking her the same question."

"I'll give her a heads-up." Kim smiled and nodded at Arlene. "While I'm here, I wanted to look at your cross-stitch kits. I could use something to do in the evenings. It sounds like I'm going to be here a while longer."

"Really?" Peggy frowned. "I thought everything was almost ready over there."

"It is, but Regina asked me to stick around and help train new hires. She usually just leaves the new manager to deal with that, but since *she's* the manager this time, she wants help." Kim rolled her eyes.

"You don't mind?" Arlene glanced at Peggy and smiled.

"Not at all. The pay is decent and I've got nothing to rush back to. I like Spicetown. The other girls are eager to get home and I won't miss any of them."

"I don't think that's why she asked you," Arlene said. "The other girls aren't hard workers."

"Yeah, well, they're young. It takes a few years to make your mistakes before you learn what's important." Kim shrugged. "And hopefully you don't do something to ruin your life along the way."

Peggy hesitated and then nodded slowly. "Are you worried that one of them might be doing that?"

Kim hunched her shoulders and sighed. "Something weird is going on over there. I just don't know what it is. I tried to talk to Regina just now, but I can tell she doesn't even notice. The chief came back a few minutes ago and took Heather. He wants Regina back at the station after we close up. We know what killed Brook now, so something else is obviously going on."

"What did Regina say?" Arlene asked as she stepped up onto the bar stool behind the counter to sit down.

"She's ignoring everything and hoping it goes away. She knows the other girls are whispering about the other death that happened a few years ago and I think they're talking about Heather, too. They don't include me, but Regina just acts like it is nothing to worry about, but I think she's wrong. When the police want to talk to you again, there's a reason for it. Usually *you* are the reason."

"Maybe he thinks Heather knows more than she's saying." Peggy's eyes shifted to Arlene, who met her gaze.

Kim looked at Arlene and then back at Peggy. "What's going on? Do you two know something I don't? Does everybody know more than I do?"

Peggy held up her hand as a calming gesture. "Not really, but we think Brook's accident is a little suspicious, too. Just like you said, it seems there might be more to it and I'm glad to hear the chief is still asking questions. It's easy to label things an accident and close the book. It sounds like he is trying to make sure that there isn't anything sinister behind it. Did you know Brook was allergic to penicillin?"

"I didn't. I don't guess anyone else over there did either, or at least, they haven't admitted to it, if they did. They've all known each other longer, though. This is my first trip."

Peggy had so many other questions, but she didn't want to sway Kim's thinking. Kim had to go back over there and work with them. "We can only hope for the best!"

"Kim, we've got several kits over here on sale if you'd like to look through them." Arlene walked over to the bin by the front door. "This brand has small beginner projects in it and it includes everything you need. It even has a teeny pair of scissors included. So cute!"

Kim laughed as she walked over to look and Peggy slipped a leash on Sully's neck for a quick walk.

Chapter 30

According to Officer Crawford, the night dispatcher, Heather had not made a sound all night. The results from the testing on the pie were already on his desk when he walked in, and Peggy had guessed right. The report said the meringue had been heavily laced with penicillin.

Conrad hung up the phone after talking things over with the county prosecutor. The search warrant had been signed. Assuming he could find the penicillin and the phone at the Nutmeg Inn, they were ready to charge Heather Halstrom for murder.

Ignoring the three telephone messages he had to call Harold Abbott back, he grabbed his hat and headed down the hallway. "Roy, you should be getting a warrant any minute now. I need you to print that out for me."

"Okay, Chief."

"And if Mr. Abbott calls back again, there's no reason to write up a phone message. You can let him know I will not be calling him back."

Roy snorted a chuckle, and Briscoe looked up at him in alarm.

"Tabor, I'm going to the Nutmeg Inn to see Heather's room. If I find what I'm looking for, I want you to reach back out to those offices in Kentucky and let them know what's happening here. They might want to take another look at their cases, too."

"Right, Chief. Did Regina show up last night?" Eugene's shift had ended just when things got interesting.

"Yeah, but she doesn't have a head for details, especially when it doesn't directly involve her. She gave me a better picture of what happened with the other two girls, though. The police reports were pretty thin and it doesn't look like either case was worked too seriously. It may be too late to fix that."

"She didn't freak out about Heather?"

"No, she seemed to only be worried she would be another employee short. She's not oozing with empathy."

Tabor shook his head. "I'd be feeling guilty for hiring her and putting the rest of my unit in danger."

"Nope. She's pretty superficial that way." Conrad shook his head. "I'm sure the thought hasn't even crossed her mind." Conrad looked over at Roy, who was watching his monitor for the warrant to come through. "Hey, Roy. What do you think about this dispatch gig? Are you liking it better now?"

"Yeah, Chief! It's actually pretty exciting. I like knowing what's going on and day shift is great. Does that mean you're going to put me back on nights?"

Conrad chuckled. "Of course not. I need to talk with Georgia and Wink before I make any decisions, but you've done a good job turning it around. I wasn't sure you were going to be a good fit, but whether you stay there or not, I think you've learned some valuable skills."

"Yeah, like treating Georgia with respect," Tabor muttered. He knew the reason the whole thing started. "Oh, yeah. I almost forgot. I found your guy, Abbott, has an outstanding warrant out on him for fraud in Maryland."

Conrad smiled. "You need to give them a call and tell them we know where he is, but that he might be leaving at any moment. See what they want us to do about it."

Tabor nodded.

"And then let Mavis Bell know. I think her instincts were right about Abbott. She thought he was trying to cheat her out of that train set in my office. She knows it's worth a lot of money and she didn't want to sell it. She thought if she didn't take his deal, he was going to steal it from her."

"If Maryland wants us to pick him up, we'll get a shoe print from him." Tabor reached for his phone.

"It's here, Chief!" Roy waved the search warrant in the air and Conrad grabbed it.

A hard rain started in the late morning with thunder and lightning threatening to end them all, so business was more than slow. Peggy cut out the pieces for Eleanor's black velvet skirt while Sully huddled under the table for added storm protection and Arlene tapped away on the laptop composing her next groundbreaking email to their customers. Once the rain let up, a flurry of customers, who had also waited out the rain, appeared needing boxes shipped and it took them both to manage them all.

When the deluge of rain and customers ended, they realized they had completely missed lunch, so Peggy ran down to the Caraway Cafe to grab whatever was left over before they closed. Wiggling through the door of the craft store with Styrofoam containers wedged under her chin, Arlene ran to help.

"What is all this?" Arlene sat the containers on the counter and began peeking inside each one. "Did you clean out the kitchen?"

Peggy laughed as she sat the rest of the cartons on the coffee table. "I think that stuff is all dessert. I've got the lunches over here."

"I'll grab us some drinks." Arlene rushed back to the storeroom and returned to the sofa. "You were gone a long time. Did they have to make us something from scratch? I guess we're lucky they didn't throw you out."

"No, we got what was left. Two specials and the desserts over there. That wasn't what delayed me. Cora Mae was sitting over there working. She went to lunch earlier and got caught in the storm, so she just stayed. That woman can work anywhere!"

"Was she working on Thanksgiving?" Arlene scowled. "I saw an ad in the paper this morning about it, and Carter Monroe is already taking credit for the whole idea. I'd be so mad if I were Cora Mae."

Carter Monroe was the president of the Bank of Spicetown and a very wealthy citizen. His wife, Delia, was living in her own version of high society, and both of them avoided interacting with the common folks. Luckily, no one missed them.

"She said he was paying for the turkeys and offered to help with promotion of the event. She knew then that he would be taking credit for it, but she seems fine with that. Carter can blow his horn all he wants. She just doesn't want Delia trying to tell her how to run the event."

"I guess Jason can run interference for her." Arlene passed a napkin to Peggy. "Did she have any Sassafras updates? There hasn't been any movement across the street today."

"Yes! She said Heather was arrested—."

"What?" Arlene interrupted. "Really? Wow, that was fast."

"Well, he found the phone and the penicillin. I don't know if she actually confessed or not, Cora didn't say that, but Heather did talk to the Chief about everything after he found the evidence. She's been transported to Paxton for some hearing they're doing in a couple of days." Cora Mae had also told Peggy that Conrad Harris appreciated what she did by sharing Mildred's information and her own observations, but she would keep that part to herself.

Arlene sighed. "It's nice to know that the drama is over. I bet the other girls go home at the end of the week. Kim is the only one that really works over there anyway. Regina would be silly to keep the other two around."

"Cora told me that the Chief thinks Heather was involved in two other deaths of co-workers. He read the reports and said Heather was on those trips, too. She has a pattern of targeting the lead. She thinks she should be the lead and if she gets them out of the way, she will get her own store."

"But you don't just kill people!" Arlene tossed her hands up. "You work harder to show the boss you can do the job."

"Well, Cora thinks maybe she didn't mean to kill them." Peggy shrugged.

"She must have known that Brook was allergic though, because you can't overdose on penicillin."

"That's true. Apparently, Heather told Brook she got penicillin for her sore throat when she went to the clinic. Brook told Heather that it gave her an itchy rash as a kid, so she just never took it again. Heather thought she'd give Brook a rash and she'd go home."

"And the other death?" Arlene waved her fork in the air. "That was a mistake, too?"

"Maybe she hit the girl on her bike and thought she'd just break a leg?" Peggy dropped her shoulders in disappointment. "I don't know."

"I'm not buying it." Arlene shook her head. "Anyone can make a mistake, but this is a pattern of murder. I hope her defense is not that she accidentally killed three people. Put me on the jury!"

Peggy laughed at Arlene's indignation. "On another note, Cora said she had been trapped in the cafe with Ross Miniken for about an hour. He had come over for lunch and stayed because of the rain, just as she had. They had a long talk."

"I'm sure he talked about himself the entire time. The man's ego fills a room." Arlene's disdain had not dissipated.

"Well, she said she'd not had a chance to get to know him yet, so I think she was glad for the time. Apparently, his wife died, and his sister-in-law is contesting the will, so he's not able to get settled in yet. They didn't have any children together and he is trying to adapt to being alone. I think he's still staying over at the Nutmeg Inn."

"I'm sure he'll be just fine. He has a winning personality and seems quite outgoing, if there is a platform where he can promote himself. I wouldn't worry about him."

"I'm sure he's going through a hard time, Arlene, and everybody navigates life changes differently. Maybe you should give him a break."

Arlene lifted one eyebrow wearily at Peggy as she took another bite.

"Cora said he asked her a lot of questions about you." Peggy intentionally chose that moment to mention this because Arlene's mouth was full, but she braced herself for Arlene's ultimate reaction.

Able only to frown, Arlene glowered at her until she swallowed. "What about me?"

Although Peggy opened her mouth to speak, Arlene cut her off.

"Oh, is he pouting because I'm not buying all the smoozy gimmicks he has? Everyone else swoons when he gives them any attention at all, and I can see right through him. He's a shallow egomaniac with no actual substance at all!"

Peggy swallowed and paused. "No, actually, that's not it."

Arlene's sneer turned into a smirk. "What is it then? What's Mr. Miniken's problem with me?"

"Cora Mae said he wants to ask you out on a date."

Do you love English Bulldogs & X-Stitch?

You can get Sully's pattern here!

https://readerlinks.com/l/4160774

What's next in the Spicetown Mysteries?~>

Celebrate Thanksgiving in Spicetown!

Coming in November....

Get your copy here!

https://readerlinks.com/l/4184543

If this is your first trip to Spicetown and you would like to see more, you can learn all about it in the original Spicetown Mystery Series.

I'd love to hear from you!

Find me on Facebook, or join my email list for upcoming news!

www.SheriRichey.com

Made in the USA
Columbia, SC
06 November 2024

45756602R00169